He was beautiful

Daphne watched Jonah walking in front of her truck with his long legs—and fabulous rear end. He was beautiful and hugely misunderstood.

She quickly unrolled her window. "I know, Jonah Closky," she said. "I know the truth about you."

He stepped toward the door, smiling. A full smile, as though he was glad that she knew. The blunt lines of his face curved, revealing something softer, something unexpected. He had dimples. And laugh lines. And of course, that imperfect tooth that other women might consider a defect but she thought was delicious.

He was delicious.

And she was in big trouble.

Dear Reader,

Wow! Here it is—the last of THE MITCHELLS OF RIVERVIEW INN series. *Worth Fighting For* has been a surprise from start to finish. It wasn't part of my original idea for the series—I didn't even know Jonah existed when I started this project. But thank goodness he did, because Daphne really needed a Mitchell boy of her own.

One of the subplots for this book was inspired by the documentary "Jamie Oliver's School Dinners." For those of you who aren't as wired to the Food Network as I am, (food porn, as my friend Sinead says) the documentary follows celebrity chef Jamie Oliver's mission to change the food British schools feed students. It's a fantastic documentary, enlightening and emotional. I highly recommend it to parents and foodies alike.

I have enjoyed this series more than I can say and I truly appreciate all the readers who have written to tell me how much they liked the books, too. Thanks so much. Now it's time to get out of the Catskills...except...Cameron is still kicking around, isn't he?

Happy reading!

Molly O'Keefe

WORTH FIGHTING FOR
Molly O'Keefe

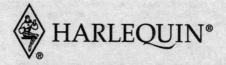

TORONTO • NEW YORK • LONDON
AMSTERDAM • PARIS • SYDNEY • HAMBURG
STOCKHOLM • ATHENS • TOKYO • MILAN • MADRID
PRAGUE • WARSAW • BUDAPEST • AUCKLAND

ISBN-13: 978-0-373-71510-7
ISBN-10:   0-373-71510-2

WORTH FIGHTING FOR

ABOUT THE AUTHOR

Molly O'Keefe has written twelve books for the Harlequin Superromance, Flipside and Duets lines. When she isn't writing happily ever after she can usually be found in the park acting as referee between her beleaguered border collie and her two-year-old son. She lives in Toronto, Canada, with her husband, son, dog and the largest heap of dirty laundry in North America.

Books by Molly O'Keefe

HARLEQUIN SUPERROMANCE

1365–FAMILY AT STAKE
1385–HIS BEST FRIEND'S BABY
1392–WHO NEEDS CUPID?
    "A Valentine for Rebecca"
1432–UNDERCOVER PROTECTOR
1460–BABY MAKES THREE*
1486–A MAN WORTH KEEPING*

HARLEQUIN FLIPSIDE

15–PENCIL HIM IN
37–DISHING IT OUT

HARLEQUIN DUETS

62–TOO MANY COOKS
95–COOKING UP TROUBLE
    KISS THE COOK

*The Mitchells of Riverview Inn

To Pam Hopkins,
I am so lucky to have you in my corner.

CHAPTER ONE

JONAH CLOSKY stared out the window and thought of money.

Great heaps of it.

He barely listened to Gary Murphy, his business partner, read over the contract. Most days he barely listened to Gary, but today Jonah was mentally counting the profit they'd make once Gary stopped reading and everyone got to the signing part.

The answer, of course, was a fortune. Plenty, for anyone else. But, for Jonah, for his plans, for Haven House, it wasn't quite enough.

It was never quite enough.

"Rick Ornus, seller, agrees to pay the cost of soil removal in the northwest corner of the property," Gary read from the sheath of papers in front of him.

Rick, who sat at the corner of the boardroom table, put up his hand, interrupting Gary. "About that," Rick said.

Jonah tuned in to the conversation with his whole body. The terms of this contract had already been hashed and rehashed. There should be no "about that's."

"Is that really necessary?" Rick asked. "That soil thing?"

"Well." Gary laid the papers down on the table, keeping his cool when Jonah knew his partner had to be having a heart attack. Gary wasn't much for "about that's," either.

"Considering the amount of arsenic in it, yes," Gary said. "It is. We will treat the rest of the property and retest, but that northwest corner needs to be dug out and all that soil replaced."

Rick looked over at Jonah and smiled. "Jonah," he said, holding out his hands, as though they were coconspirators. "Come on. Between us. You know that with the right amount of money Barringer will overlook that—"

"I don't bribe city officials," Jonah said. "And I don't build on dirty land."

"What about your current site?" Rick asked. "I heard you were about to start building and the city just shut you down for poisoned soil."

"Where'd you hear that?" Gary asked and Jonah nearly hung his head at his partner's transparency. It was no wonder Gary couldn't play cards—a ten-year-old child had a better poker face.

"Everyone knows," Rick said. "Yesterday, I must have gotten seven calls from people telling me about it. It'll be all over the papers in no time."

Gary's worried gaze flicked to Jonah and Jonah held up a hand, trying to get his business partner to relax, to not fly off the handle like some freaked-out howler monkey.

"So," Rick continued, his eyes gleaming with a certain smug satisfaction. "Why don't you guys cut the righteous environmental act—"

"Act?" Gary nearly squealed and Jonah rolled his eyes.

"Yeah, and we can get down to business," Rick said. "You guys have a good racket going pretending to clean up all this bad land, but obviously—"

Well, crap, Jonah thought. *Now I'm offended.*

And the estimated revenue from this project that he'd just totaled in his head went back to zero.

"There will be no business," Jonah said, leaning forward.

"What do you mean?" Rick asked. "We're ready to sign the papers—" Rick looked at Gary, who had seen this kind of scenario enough to know the ending. Gary simply leaned back and tossed the unsigned contract in the garbage.

"What are you doing?" Rick cried.

A long time ago Jonah had made the promise that he'd do whatever he had to do to get the job done, but he wouldn't explain himself and he wouldn't beg. And while he might have to do business with rats like Rick, he'd make sure the rats always knew he wasn't one of them.

"I'm not sure what the problem is here, gentlemen," Rick said, looking far less smug and a little more sweaty. "You need the land, I can sell it to you. And we can all make a bunch of money if you just forget this soil problem. It's not like you haven't done it before."

"We're done," Jonah said, standing so fast the chair spun backward and hit the floor-to-ceiling windows of his boardroom. "Get out."

"Come on, Jonah. I'm sure we can—"

"We can't," Jonah said, striding to the door, opening it and nodding to Katie, who sat at the front desk. "Notify security," he told her.

"You know—" Rick's face became bitter and Jonah crossed his arms over his chest and waited for the guy to hammer the nails in his own coffin "—you're getting a pretty nasty reputation, Jonah. Between the number of real estate agents ready to stab you in the back and that failed soil test on your current site, pretty soon no one is going to be willing to sit down with you."

A week ago, Rat-faced Rick had been so relieved that Jonah wanted to buy the land with the arsenic problem, that Rick had agreed to Jonah's terms, including the soil removal.

But then they'd failed that soil test—and apparently the whole world knew about it, and Jonah's delicate balancing act was in jeopardy.

"Let me tell you what you've just done, Rick," Jonah said. "Not only is our deal over, but I am going to make sure that you will be unable to sell that disgusting property you're lying to everyone about. And you won't be able to make a land sale in New Jersey ever again."

Rick glanced over to Gary, who only shrugged. "You screwed yourself when you assumed we were like you, Rick," Gary told him point-blank, which was what Gary was good for.

Rick gaped like a fish and Gary sighed, coming to his feet. "Go, Rick," he said, "before Jonah decides to throw you out himself."

Rick glanced between them and finally, grabbing his twenty-year-old briefcase and equally ancient trench coat, he left, taking Jonah's profit margin on the condos with him.

"Someone else is going to get that land," Gary said, turning to stare out the window, across the river at the Manhattan skyline. He took off his glasses, cleaned them on the corner of his rumpled madras shirt then put them back on. "Someone who isn't going to deal with that arsenic problem. And they'll pay off Barringer and the inspectors and build a school there or something all because you couldn't control your temper with some scumbag." He sighed and Jonah felt bad, for Gary's sake. He took these things too hard.

"No," Jonah assured his partner of ten years. "They

won't." He leaned out the door. "Katie, please get me David Printer at the *Times*." He needed to find out if the soil test results were going public. They needed to do as much financial damage control as possible.

Katie nodded and went to work on the phone. Jonah walked back into the boardroom, letting the door shut behind him.

"That soil test hurt us, Jonah. We've never failed one before," Gary said, running his hands through his haywire brown hair. "Thank God we hadn't started building yet. That would be a nightmare."

"We'll retreat the soil and retest in three weeks. We'll put out the press release and it will all blow over. We'll be building by the end of May." Barring any more disasters in the next two months.

"If this goes public—" Gary looked at him from the corner of his eye.

"It won't."

"But if it does? Can you imagine the calls from tenants from other buildings wondering if their children are going to grow up infertile? Or if they are all going to get cancer." Gary rested his head against the glass. "We're going to lose the funding for Haven House, I know we are."

"No," Jonah said, perhaps a bit too stridently. A bit too surely. That fragile dream would be protected, at all costs. "We won't."

"I should have been a dentist. I don't know why I let you talk me out of that."

"Because dentists are boring," Jonah said, bored of this conversation. The conference-room phone buzzed and Jonah sat as he hit the intercom button.

"David," he said, "I don't know what you've heard—"

"It's not David." His mother's voice crackled through the speakerphone and Jonah, who in deep, scary places he didn't acknowledge was worried Gary was right, felt the dark pallor of his conference room lift.

"Mom," he cried and picked up the handset as Gary grabbed his stuff and left the room to give Jonah some privacy. "I tried calling last night—"

"I was at Sheila's," she said and Jonah could hear the weariness in her voice and wished he could throw it out the way he did Rick. Or absorb it right over the phone. Every heavy load and worry that crossed his mother's path he would gladly add to his own weight.

"How is Aunt Sheila?" His mother's best friend had earned the honorary title of *aunt* twenty-five years ago when she'd nursed him through the chicken pox.

"She's doing great. She had me over for dinner, a fancy thing she had catered in celebration of the doctor's clean bill of health."

Jonah sat back in his chair and smiled, feeling better than he had in weeks. "That's good news," he said. "Amazing news."

"Yes." He heard the smile in his mother's voice. "It is."

"We should all celebrate," he said, thinking of his schedule. "Maybe a trip at the end of the summer. South of France? We can lie on a beach—"

"That sounds wonderful, honey, but I'm calling about something else."

Jonah spun his chair to face the window and lifted his boot up to rest on the corner of the table. "All right, what's up?"

Iris sighed.

Jonah knew his mother as well and as totally as any boy could know his mom and he read bad news in that sigh. "What's going on?" he asked. Jonah didn't fear much. He was reckless with his career, with his money, with his body, but he lived in fear of something happening to his mother.

"Jonah, last winter, when I told you Sheila and I were on vacation, it wasn't really the truth. I was in New York…at the Riverview Inn."

His gut went cold at the name. His brothers' inn. Where his father lived. The brothers he never knew. And the father he didn't want to know.

"And I'm going back. Today."

"What?" he asked, stunned. "Why?"

"Because it's time," she said. "It's time for both of us to deal with this."

"Mom, you tried to deal with it thirty years ago, remember?" he asked, cruelly reminding her of the situation with her husband in the hopes that it might change her mind. "You wrote to him twice. And twice Patrick told you he didn't want us."

"He didn't want *me,* Jonah. It had nothing to do with you. And he wants terribly to meet you now."

"Well, now is thirty years too late. I think I've made my feelings clear about this, Mom."

"I know, but—"

He groaned and tipped his head against the high back of his chair. He'd made a promise with his first million dollars—a promise he'd actually made at the age of sixteen while he watched his mother clean houses and pretend to be happy—that he'd never say no to her.

Whatever she asked for he would do.

And so, being his mother, she'd made a point of never

asking for anything. But he had a sense that was all going to change.

"I am asking you to come, Jonah. I am asking you to meet your father. To give your brothers a chance."

He could financially destroy the competition. He could intimidate shady inspectors and city officials. He'd strong-armed the Mafia off his building sites.

But he couldn't say no to his mother.

"When?" He sighed.

"As soon as you can make it," she said, and he could hear her smile, her joy—so fleeting—flooding over the phone and he smiled wearily.

"I need a few days," he told her, thinking of his schedule. A few days and then he'd come face-to-face with the family that, sight unseen, he loathed.

DAPHNE LARSON, the early spring sunshine in her eyes, pulled the boxes of herbs out of the bed of her truck and staggered to the kitchen door of the Riverview Inn.

She expected, any moment now, for the kitchen door to open and the men of the Riverview to flood out to help her.

The door stayed closed and the boxes just got heavier.

So, unable to open the door herself without dropping her load, she used her head to knock lightly on the window.

"Oh, for crying out loud," Alice Mitchell, executive chef of the inn, said, opening the door. She was married to Gabe Mitchell, the owner, and had, in the past year, become Daphne's closest friend. "Knocking with your head? What's wrong with you?"

"My delivery guy quit," Daphne explained, sliding the boxes onto the counter already crowded with bowls of fruits and vegetables ready to be used for the day's menus.

"Again?"

"Again," Daphne said, bending backward slightly to relieve the pinch in her lower back.

"Why don't you go in and see Delia," Alice said, referring to the massage therapist with the magic fingers who also happened to be dating Max Mitchell, Gabe's brother. "She doesn't have any bookings for the rest of the morning."

"I wish I could," Daphne said, brushing her long blond braid over her shoulder. "But you're my last delivery and we've got the first crop of asparagus coming up, so I should get back."

"Well, have some tea at least," Alice offered.

It smelled so good in the Riverview kitchen. Like delicious things baking and calories. Daphne swore she gained a pound just sitting next to one of Alice's pies.

"I'd love some tea," Daphne agreed, willing to risk some osmosis weight gain for the chance to sit. And perhaps to talk to Tim, Alice's assistant, if she could get him alone. "You don't know anyone looking for a job, do you? A kid from one of Max's after-school programs or something?"

Alice shook her head and stepped back to her spot at the counter rolling pastry dough.

"We're having the same problem." Tim brought her a glass of mint iced tea. She tried to catch his eyes, but he set down the glass on the counter next to her and was gone, back across the room to the peppers he was chopping. She had a highly uncomfortable question to ask him, and she needed an answer today. "Not enough staff," he said, studying the peppers as though he knew she was here to talk to him.

"Are you sure you should even be working?" Daphne asked Alice, settling in for some good kitchen chitchat. No one did kitchen chitchat like Alice. And maybe if Daphne stayed long enough, Tim would relax his guard and she'd catch him alone. "It's only been a month—"

Alice rolled her eyes. "You are worse than Gabe. It's been a month and a half. I had a baby, not a leg amputation. And I'm just rolling pastry."

"Okay." Daphne took a sip of tea. "If you want to be out here working when you could be in your bed sleeping, that's your business."

"Trust me," Alice groused. "There's not much sleeping."

Daphne laughed. She remembered those early months of Helen's life with such heart-squeezing nostalgia. The nursing and napping, the late-night feedings, the exhaustion and sore breasts. It was a very special kind of torture. And she'd do it all over again in a heartbeat.

"Where is everyone?" Daphne asked, hoisting herself onto a stool in the corner. Usually the place was packed with family members and employees, but today it was practically a ghost town.

"Jonah's supposed to be arriving today," Alice said and Daphne's mouth fell open.

"Really? Today?"

"Apparently he called this morning," Alice said and took a bowl of raspberry preserves and began to spread a thick layer over the pastry. "Everyone has found some reason to be out front when he arrives. I swear Gabe has trimmed the bushes to within an inch of their life."

"So why aren't you out there?" Daphne asked. *She* wanted to go out there and wait for the man's appearance.

Gabe and Max's mother had vanished thirty years ago only to reappear a few months ago with the heartbreaking news that Gabe and Max had another brother they'd never known about.

That Patrick had another son.

Jonah.

Iris had gone home to help nurse a friend through her last round of chemo and had returned over a week ago with the news that Jonah was planning to come to the inn.

The whole family had been jumping like dogs in a thunderstorm ever since. And the later he was, the more everyone jumped.

Soap operas couldn't compete with what was happening at the Riverview Inn.

"I don't think he's coming," Alice said, shaking a black curl out of her eyes. "I think the guy gets off on leading this family on. He's postponed three times over the past two weeks and I swear Patrick is going to have a heart attack. And Iris…" She shook her head.

Daphne nodded in total understanding. Iris was bordering on tragic. Iris, with her dramatic black and silver hair and dark eyes, seemed so sad to Daphne. As if she lived every day with her mistakes, taking them out for polishing to be worn around her neck. Never forgetting and never letting anyone else forget, either.

"Iris is terrified everyone is going to hate everyone else," Alice said. "And, she's probably right."

"How is Gabe taking this?" Daphne asked. Max was fairly sanguine about Jonah coming. Patrick was nearly rabid with eagerness, but Gabe…not so much.

"Gabe is ready to pounce if Jonah so much as looks at Patrick cross-eyed." Alice shook her head and rolled the pastry into ruglach. "It's like he's a four-year-old and someone is trying to steal his favorite toy."

"It's a tricky situation," Daphne said. She couldn't even imagine what it would be like to come face-to-face with a son you never knew you had. A son who might not like you. Or vice versa.

"Hey," Alice said, turning to Daphne and changing the subject. "I see Sven's put that land up for sale."

Daphne rolled her eyes. Her neighbor, Sven Lungren, and his land were a reoccurring bad dream in her life. About once a year he put the land up for sale and she offered what she could for it and he kept saying no. But he never sold it to anyone else and she wasn't sure if the reason was that no one met his mysterious price, or that he was going through the exercise to taunt her.

All she knew was that if she got his acreage, she could expand. The existing Athens Organics land was being used to maximum output. She was rotating crops as much as she could, but the demand for her organic fruits and vegetables was beginning to overwhelm what she could supply with her little patch of property.

Plus she had dreams of expanding her small apple grove into a full-on pick-your-own apple orchard. That required land. And money. And a few years to come to fruition, but Daphne was thinking big these days.

"I gave him my offer yesterday," Daphne said. "I haven't heard."

"Well, good luck," Alice said with a grim smile.

The sound of baby Stella fussing buzzed from the baby monitor tucked into one of the pots that hung from the ceiling, and Daphne's entire body practically spasmed with longing. Hormones flooded her bloodstream and her heart chugged—baby, baby, baby, baby.

At thirty-seven Daphne's biological clock was in hyper-drive and she wished she could tell her body that a baby wasn't going to happen, that it could stop with the hormonal fanfare. But she couldn't and so her womb set up a howl when she held Stella or heard her sleepy cry over the monitor.

Alice paused, listened then went to the sink to wash her hands. "That's a real cry," she said. "I better go feed her. I'll talk to you later."

Daphne waved goodbye. Finally it was just her and Tim in the kitchen. She prepared herself for some hard-core begging.

"Forget it, Daphne," he said, before she could even open her mouth. "I'm not going."

"Tim." She sighed. "You haven't even heard—"

"I don't have to." He turned to face her, pushing up his black glasses with his wrist. "I've been to two tedious functions with you in the past month."

"Oh, come on. They weren't that tedious," she argued, knowing this was a losing battle. Political fund-raising events were boring. In fact, she'd learned they were the definition of boring. But she'd promised her ex, Jake, she'd go. Still there was no way she'd be going alone.

"This one is for the local school board," she said. "A family-style picnic. You love picnics."

"I hate picnics," Tim practically cried. "Look, if it's so important for your ex-husband's political aspirations that you be there, why don't you go as his date?"

Daphne shot him a look, making it clear that she'd really rather eat glass than go as Jake's date.

"Then don't go," Tim said, scooping up his pile of peppers and dumping them into a bowl.

"I promised," she said, as if it were that simple. In some ways it was. She had made the promise in the middle of the night eight months ago, while her ex-husband sat at her kitchen table and pretended not to stare at her legs under her T-shirt. That's probably why she'd said yes, she'd been drunk off his sideways glances.

It had been eons since anyone had glanced at her, sideways or not.

But there were other, not as simple reasons she was helping Jake.

"Besides," Tim said, crumbling a big block of feta over the peppers, "I hate to break it to you, sweetheart, but pretending to be your love interest isn't fooling anyone. Three guys asked me out at that Democrats For a Living Planet event last week."

"Really?" she asked, slightly stunned. She'd thought their act was fairly convincing.

"Really." He nodded.

Daphne sighed, she knew a losing battle when she was in one.

"Anyone good?" she asked, pleased for her friend, even if he was dumping her.

"Yep." His eyes twinkled. "As much as I'd love an excuse to go to some family picnic, Daph, I'm just too busy and frankly, I'm just too gay."

She laughed and slung her arm over his shoulder in order to kiss his cheek. "It's too bad all the other men around here are married," she said. "Or as good as," she added, thinking of Max and Delia. There was a lot of good-natured betting going on regarding when Max would get around to asking the fiery redhead to marry him. If he did it before the end of summer this year, Daphne was going to be the big winner.

"Married or gay," Tim joked and waggled his dark eyebrows at her.

"Excuse me," a deep voice interrupted their laughter. Daphne and Tim twirled to the back door where a tall, dark and very handsome man stood, silhouetted in the bright morning sunlight.

Good gravy, she thought as her biological clock started its usual ruckus around handsome men of a certain age. Her womb was suddenly the overeager kid in class waving its hand screaming, "Me! Pick me!"

He was too good-looking to be real.

The stranger's black T-shirt and blue jeans were the kind of casual clothes that looked more expensive than the finest suit. Or maybe it was the world-class body beneath them that made them look so good.

Daphne was suddenly very aware of her dirty gray chinos and work boots.

"Can I help you?" Tim asked casually, as if Brad Pitt's younger, taller, darker brother walked into his kitchen every day.

She could barely breathe, much less talk.

The mystery man slid his trendy aviator sunglasses up on his forehead and Daphne was struck by the sense that she knew this guy. She'd seen him somewhere. And she knew something about him. Something bad.

Where had she seen him?

He stepped out of the doorway and the glare of the sun, and suddenly she remembered. His face had been all over the front page of the *Times* a week ago. He built condos on polluted land.

"I'm—"

"The Dirty Developer," she said, snapping her fingers as it all came together. "That's where I've seen you."

As soon as the words fell from her imprudent lips she

wished she could suck them back. She actually had to fight to keep her hand from slapping over her mouth. Tim pinched her and the Dirty Developer's jaw tightened as waves of hostility rolled off him and pounded her right in the chest.

"I'm Jonah Closky," he said and slid his glasses back over his eyes. "And I'm leaving."

CHAPTER TWO

AND YET ANOTHER excellent example of my big mouth, Daphne thought, as the door swung shut behind Jonah.

"That's the missing Mitchell?" Tim asked into the stone silence of the kitchen then whistled low. "You scared him off good. You better apologize."

"To the Dirty Developer?" she cried; her skin practically crawled at the thought.

"To Patrick's son," Tim said and she groaned. He was right.

Daphne took off after the Dirty Developer/the missing Mitchell boy/the handsomest man she'd seen in real life.

You'd think by this point she'd have learned to think before she opened her mouth. But as Jake had always told her, it was as though she came with a broken edit mechanism. And a temper that didn't really understand the phrase "appropriate time and place."

Though she could usually control that.

"Hey!" she yelled at Jonah's very wide retreating back as she chased him to his Jeep. The gravel of the parking lot crunched under her boots.

The guy's angry stride made it impossible to catch up to him, and before she knew it he was pulling open the driver-side door of his dusty vehicle.

She bumped her fast walk into a jog. If she actually chased away Patrick's missing son, she'd never forgive herself. To say nothing of probably losing her biggest client and best friends.

"Hey wait!"

Finally he whirled, squinting against the sun behind her. At least she hoped he was squinting against the sun and not glaring at her as though she were some bug buzzing around his head. "I'm so sorry," she said, coming to stop a few feet from him. "That was very inappropriate. I never expected you to come in the back door. Everyone is waiting for you up at the front, which really is a terrible reason for saying something so rude. So, I apologize. Again. More, actually. I apologize more. If that's possible."

She just didn't know when to shut up.

He watched her for a second, all that handsome male focused right on her and, despite the sunglasses that covered his eyes and his barely contained animosity, she felt her stomach dip as if she were going down a hill too fast.

Whew. He was some kind of man.

And then he shrugged.

She apologized and he shrugged.

For the life of her she didn't know how to respond to that shrug.

He was destroying the planet and he was rude, to boot. This guy didn't deserve the Mitchells. But that wasn't her call.

Best foot forward, take two.

"I'm Daphne Larson, Athens Organics. Your family will be out here shortly I'm sure. Everyone's thrilled you're here."

Jonah looked at her hand as if she were offering him a palm full of manure. A smile—or was it a sneer—tugged at the corner of his mouth. She couldn't really be sure without seeing his eyes. He pulled his keys from his pocket and scanned the lawn behind her, utterly ignoring her hand.

"Tell my mom to call me on my cell," he said and turned to his Jeep.

Wow, she thought, stunned by the audacity of his rudeness. In her world no one treated anyone the way this man had the balls to treat her.

She gritted her teeth.

"Jonah." She reached out and put a hand on his arm, just below the sleeve of his T-shirt and the spark between his sun-warmed flesh and her rough hand shocked both of them. She jerked her hand back and shook it, uncomfortable by the contact and the spark that zinged through her whole body.

Women like her didn't know anything about men like him.

"Your family—" She tried again, distracted by the tingle in her arm.

He ripped off his sunglasses and waves of anger poured from him as if it had been contained by those expensive shades. For the second time in the mere moments she'd been in his presence she fought for a big breath. This man wasn't rude, he was mad. And he was barely in control.

His whole body radiated fury.

"Don't call them that," he said, his voice a burning purr. His face might as well have been made of stone. "They're not family."

"Then why are you here?" she blurted, stunned. "If you feel that way—"

He made a dismissive gesture, his lips thin and white. Conversation, his vibe screamed, over.

Now she was getting a little mad.

"Look, I just wanted to apologize about the Dirty Developer thing—"

"Are you *trying* to piss me off?"

"No," she clarified. "I'm trying to apologize."

"Well, how about you start by not calling me that?"

If he hadn't used that tone with her, maybe she could have kept her mouth shut. "I didn't," she said, arching her eyebrows. "The *New York Times* did. If you don't like the title, maybe you should rethink your business practices."

Not a very good apology. She could see that. Now. Now that he was angry all over again and she was a little peeved herself.

"Athens Organics?" he asked, tilting his head, his blue eyes sharp, as if he could see right through her, past her pink chambray shirt and the T-shirt bra with the fraying strap, down to her bones, her DNA. And he judged all of it, all of her, as somehow beneath him.

"Let me guess, you grow a few tomatoes?" he asked. "Sell them on the roadside?"

"Athens Organics is a thirty-acre, environmentally sound organic farm."

"You grow a lot of tomatoes," he said, but it wasn't a compliment. This man, in his fancy clothes and his bad attitude, understood one thing. Money.

And she only worked for one reason: to be able to look herself in the mirror and smile every day. To be able to pass on the best possible earth to her daughter.

She took a deep breath. "I employ thirty people and give them a fair wage. I support my daughter and myself and I am proud of what I do. I haven't sold myself, or this planet, to do it." She studied him. "How about you?" she asked. "Are you proud of what you do?"

He didn't answer, not that she expected him to. He simply stood there, staring at her until, because she was who she was, her righteous temper flickered and died and she suddenly felt the need to apologize again. As if she'd done something wrong.

She opened her mouth, mustering up the energy for one more sorry to this loathsome man.

"Yes," he told her. "I am."

Her mouth hung open, stunned. Building homes on dirty, poisoned land. He was proud of that?

"Your father is going to be so disappointed in you," she whispered. He stepped toward her so fast she almost fell back. She almost put up her hand, not to ward him off, but to push back. The man was too much. Too angry. Too resentful.

"I have no father," he said, each word like a bullet from a gun.

"Son?" Patrick Mitchell, as if summoned, appeared on the other side of the Jeep. He wiped his hand across his large chest, like a nervous boy. His heart was all too visible in his watery blue eyes.

Eyes that were, she realized, just like Jonah's.

No, she wanted to cry. *No, Patrick, don't put your hopes on this man. Don't let him hurt you, because he will.*

She knew it in her bones.

This man hurt everyone.

"JONAH?" Patrick asked again, waiting for the big man to turn away from Daphne. The air crackled between her and the stranger with Iris's jawline and hair color, who could only be his youngest son. Patrick could tell she was upset but he was too at loose ends to try to determine what had happened.

Christ, he couldn't even figure out what to do with his hands. His heart was thundering in his chest and all he wanted to do was pull that man, that boy he never got to know into his arms and hold him as tight as he could.

My son, his whole body cried. *That's my son.*

Daphne stepped away from Jonah, keeping her eyes on him as though he were a snake that might strike. Crossing in front of the Jeep, she stepped up to Patrick and wrapped her sturdy arms around him. He watched Jonah's stiff back sag momentarily.

What is happening here? Patrick wondered.

"You're a good man," Daphne whispered in his ear. Stunned, he tried to tilt his head, to push away slightly so he could see her face, but she held on tight. "The very best. I would have killed for a father like you." She kissed his cheek, patted his chest and walked away.

Sparing one sharp glance over her shoulder at Jonah.

Odd, Patrick thought, curious about what had gotten into their practical fruit and vegetable supplier.

He looked at Jonah to find the young man watching him. Staring at him across five feet and thirty-plus years. Jonah wore his sunglasses and Patrick longed to tell him to take them off. To let him see his eyes. They were blue, Iris had said, like Patrick's own.

"Hi," Patrick finally said into the tense silence between them. Jonah nodded, a regal tilt to his head and Patrick felt more unsure than he had the morning after his wife had walked away, leaving him with two young boys to care for.

The speeches he'd prepared and discarded over the past few months couldn't be resurrected. He didn't remember anything he'd thought would be so prudent to say. All those things that would explain the past thirty years without casting blame or judging. All the words he'd hoped would bridge the gap between them vanished. His brain was empty.

What should I say? he wondered, jamming his hands in his pockets. *What am I supposed to do with my hands? Why doesn't Jonah say something? Why doesn't he take off those damn glasses?*

Jonah just stood there.

"I'm glad you're here," Patrick said. It was a ridiculous understatement. A mere patch on what he truly felt, as if his life, missing something for so long, was finally going to come together. And this boy, his boy, this strong, handsome and angry man was the key to it all.

But Jonah stared at him as though Patrick were speaking French and he didn't understand the language.

"Son—"

"Where's my mother?" Jonah asked, his voice flat.

"She went back to her cabin to freshen up," Patrick said, stammering slightly. He understood it wasn't going to be roses with this boy. They had a lot of demons between them that needed to be put to rest. But he had hoped for a better start. Something closer to friendly than this frigid behavior. Iris had warned him that Jonah was not happy about this. That he was reluctant to come. But Patrick truly had not expected there to be no connection. They were flesh and blood after all and it wasn't as though Patrick had known about him and rejected him. If he'd known Iris was pregnant when she left, he would have moved heaven and earth to get them back.

"I'm sure she'll be out here soon. My boys are coming, too. Gabe just had a baby and he'll want to show her—"

"Listen…Patrick," Jonah said, his voice cutting him like a knife. "I'm not here for a family reunion. I'm here because my mother asked me to be here. And—" his voice grew slightly meaner, mocking "—you probably don't remember this about my mom but she doesn't ask for much. So, I'm here for her. I don't care about your sons—"

"They are your brothers," Patrick insisted.

"They are no one," Jonah said. "You are all strangers and you're going to stay that way."

Patrick watched this boy and tried to see into him, tried to find him amongst all that attitude. But couldn't. And it broke his heart a little.

"We'll see about that," Patrick said, not ready to give up the fight just yet.

Jonah shook his head. "This isn't a made-for-TV movie, Patrick. There is no happy ending for us. Mom had no business trying to get us all together."

"Don't you want her to be happy?" Patrick asked.

Jonah lifted his sunglasses before bracing himself against his Jeep. Patrick felt pinned by the hate in his son's blue eyes. Eyes that were, as Iris had said, identical to his own.

"You don't know my mom," Jonah said. "You don't know what makes her happy. And you sure as hell don't know me."

"I want to," Patrick said, bracing himself against the Jeep, too. There was only so much of this man's disdain and disrespect he could take. "You are my son and I want to be a part of your life."

"Well." Jonah laughed and the sound made Patrick wince. "You should have thought of that thirty years ago when you told your wife you wanted nothing to do with her. Twice." Jonah put his glasses back on and checked his watch, dismissing Patrick like a waiter at a restaurant. "Tell my mom I'll pick her up for lunch—"

"Tell her yourself." Iris appeared on the walkway leading from the cabin she'd been staying in. She wore red—a scarf in her hair and a banner of crimson across her lips. Happiness, a certain motherly excitement radiated from her like raw electricity. It was as if the woman Patrick had gotten to reknow in the past five months was plugged in suddenly, amped up.

She looked like the woman he'd married. The woman he fell in love with so long ago. And seeing that woman again knocked all the wind right out of him.

He barely stopped himself from sagging to the ground.

"Hey, Mom!" Jonah said, his face changing, growing younger, lighter, happier. His body, so rigid, softened as he picked up the smiling Iris and wrapped her in a giant bear hug.

"It's been too long," Jonah said.

"Yes," Iris agreed. She stroked her son's hair away from his face and pulled off his sunglasses. "That's better," she said, smiling into his eyes.

Patrick felt as if he'd been punched in the gut.

They were a unit, these two. A family. Who was he, at this point in their lives, to insist on being involved?

There was so little chance of this working, he realized. He understood Jonah's anger and Iris's reticence to get him and Jonah under the same roof.

"Well, well." Gabe, his oldest boy, stepped up next to Patrick while Max, his middle son, flanked him. Patrick could not have been more relieved.

This was *his* unit. *His* family.

"I should have guessed that Jonah would use Mom's maiden name, but I never put two and two together," Gabe murmured quietly so Jonah and Iris didn't hear. "The Dirty Developer is our missing brother."

Patrick's jaw dropped. "No," he breathed. "No way." They'd talked about the news article this morning over coffee and he hadn't put two and two together, either.

But Jonah did bear a remarkable resemblance to the grainy picture of the man in the newspaper.

My son? Patrick thought. *Someone with my blood was capable of such things?*

It was obscene. Gross.

"Jonah," Iris said, keeping her arm around him but pointing him toward Patrick and the boys. "Meet your brothers."

Max stepped forward, all business, a policeman to the core. "Max," he said, holding out his hand. "Good to meet you."

Jonah just stared at the hand and Patrick held his breath, waiting for Max's short fuse to be lit by Jonah's apparent ingrained disrespect. The last thing this situation needed was Max's fighting instincts to be stirred.

"Jonah," Iris admonished the full grown man next to her as though he were a five-year-old. Jonah reached out to shake Max's hand.

"And I'm Gabe," Gabe said, stepping up beside his brothers. With all of them standing together Patrick could see how similar they all were. Tall men, like him. Gabe had Patrick's blond hair and olive skin. Max and Jonah had Iris's dramatic coloring—dark hair and light skin—though Max's eyes were dark. And Jonah's eyes, like Gabe's, were blue.

Patrick glanced at Iris and caught the worry in her expression, her clenched hands and tight lips.

The parking lot was filled with dangerous fumes, combustible tempers and incredibly hurt feelings. The wrong word uttered and Patrick knew the whole place would go up in smoke. But he didn't know what to say. What to do. This whole situation was too big to be dealt with. How did one pull it apart and try to fix what was so terribly wrong?

"Well, now," Iris said, charging into the clutch of boys, wrapping her arm around Jonah's waist and grabbing Max's hand, giving them both a little jostle. She glanced around, her smile fierce, her eyes daring any one of them to say something wrong at this moment. "Isn't this nice."

Patrick tipped his head back and laughed.

That's how, he thought, pride and respect for Iris washing over him. *That's how you do it.*

IRIS COULD BE a powerful riptide, dragging Jonah places he didn't want to go. School. Church. Parties. Into the Riverview Inn for lunch.

"Go," he told her when she turned to wait for him. Patrick, Max and Gabe had already headed for the front doors. Max and Gabe had practically grabbed the laughing Patrick and ran away with him, as if rescuing him from Jonah. "I'll be right in."

This was not my idea, Jonah wanted to yell. But he didn't have enough air. He didn't have enough air to walk to the lodge, much less give those men, his brothers, the fight everyone was itching to get to.

My chest, he thought, a frenzied panic starting to claw up his back.

"Mom," he said when she continued to stare at him with her obsidian eyes, knowing him far too well to believe him. She thought he was going to turn and run.

"I have to call Gary," he lied. "A quick call and I'll be right in."

She quirked an eyebrow and he smiled, dug into his pocket and chucked her his car keys, which she caught deftly in one hand the way she used to when he was a teenager.

Go, he wanted to beg, *please just go.*

"Happy?" he asked and immediately knew it was the wrong thing to say. Her eyes got wet and she bit her lower lip.

"I am, Jonah," she said, standing against the rustic and wooded background of the inn like a brave and noble pioneer woman. Which so suited how he always saw her. Strong and stalwart. Unflinching but also, most of the time, unsmiling.

Life had been hard on Mom.

"I am very happy right now," she said and Jonah forced himself to smile so she would leave him for a few minutes.

Just a few was all he needed. Or he'd pass out on the gravel.

His body awash in cold sweat, he waited until she worked her way down the path to the lodge before he opened his passenger car door and slumped into the seat. Gasping, he pawed open the glove compartment and grabbed his emergency inhaler.

It had been weeks since he'd needed this. Weeks since the asthma had fought past his carefully acquired relaxation tools.

He took a deep puff from the inhaler. Another. Waited, inhaler poised, until finally, he felt the steroids at work, opening his lungs. His throat.

Air, like cold, clean water, filled his body, and his head stopped spinning.

He stared at the brilliant blue sky, the muscular shoulders of the Catskill Mountains and waited for his body, his constant betrayer, to fall into line.

"See you later, Tim!" The tall blonde, Daphne, shut the kitchen door behind her and stepped onto the gravel heading toward her white pickup truck with the Athens Organics logo in green on the side.

But she stopped, like a deer sensing danger and glanced over at the Jeep, the open door and him slouching in his passenger seat.

God, she was pretty.

Her hair, so gold it seemed white, was lit like a halo around her head, as if further proof of the differences between them. He could practically feel the devil's horns pushing out from his skull. Her green eyes raked him. Her lush mouth opened slightly in surprise and, he was sure, a mild disgust.

Not wanting her to see him like this, he tossed the inhaler back in the glove box and sat up. Met her gaze as if he had nothing to hide.

She lifted a hand—a farewell or a greeting he didn't know—then walked to her truck, got in and drove away, right past him, without another glance.

CHAPTER THREE

JONAH HAD SAT THROUGH more than his share of tough negotiations. He could sit unfazed through the heaviest, stoniest
of silences, smiling slightly until the opposition cracked.

It was a skill he'd picked up from the many hours Aunt
Sheila spent with him playing Stare Down during that
chicken pox incident.

But even he had to admit that lunch was rough. Rough
in the way the Nuremberg Trial was rough. Rough like the
South surrendering to the North. Civilized on the surface
but only one wrong word away from an all-out brawl.

"That wasn't so bad, was it?" Mom asked, resting her
head against his shoulder, while linking her arm through
his. He was walking her from the lodge to her cottage
across the clearing that was filled with the electric-green
of a new spring. He slid on his sunglasses against the blaze
of the sun.

He had to admit, much like the meal he hadn't eaten and
the room he didn't eat it in, the place was nice.

That was all he was going to admit.

"It was pretty bad." He laughed, putting his hand over
hers and holding it tightly.

"Well, you didn't help," she chastised him. "Sitting
there like some kind of—"

"What?"

"I don't know. Tough guy."

"I am a tough guy," he protested.

"Please," she said. "You barely said two words."

"They talked plenty," he reminded her. Had they ever. Alice and Delia, the redheaded Texan, could talk paint off a wall. They were like two birds—bright and pretty but chattering constantly. He'd tuned them out until one of them mentioned Daphne, then like some kind of radar, he tuned right in.

Idiot, he thought.

"Max and Gabe barely said two words," she said, seeming preoccupied.

"Gabe said enough," he assured her. Gabe, when everyone was occupied with passing dishes and spooning out salad and cooing at the black-haired, squashed-face baby, had turned to him, eyebrow arched in a way Jonah completely understood and said, "Dirty Developer?"

He'd pushed away from the table for one wild moment, ready to put his fist in Gabe's smug face but Max put a hand between them and said, "It would break Iris's and Dad's hearts if you fought."

It had been the appropriate bucket of cold water. But still, Jonah felt that anger in his stomach. The anger remarkably similar to the one that had fueled him for years on the playground when kids called him shrimp or tiny tunes or baby.

But he did hope that before he left he might get a chance to have a quick conversation with Gabe Mitchell. The kind of conversation that might end in a bloody nose.

"So, are you satisfied?" he asked, glancing down at her. "Family reunited so we can all get on with our lives."

She stopped and stared at him, her dark eyes like spotlights on his grimy little soul. "I know this is hard for you, Jonah—"

He laughed and tugged her into motion. "No, it's not hard at all," he clarified. "It's not hard because I have no expectations, Mom." He knew this was going to hurt, but she'd clearly gone slightly delusional since coming here over the winter. Maybe it was grief and stress over Aunt Sheila's battles, but his mom wasn't thinking clearly. "I have no attachment to these men." When he saw her shaking her head, he spun her to face him. He took off his glasses so she could see how serious he was. "These men don't mean anything to me. And they are never going to. I don't want anything from them, or need anything from them."

She searched his eyes and he let her. This was his truth. "You are what matters to me," he told her and she smiled. But it was one of her sad smiles.

"Oh, honey." She sighed, cupping his cheek. "You're what matters to me, too. That's why I want you here. Why I want you to stay."

"Mom—"

"Look," she interrupted. "Everyone in there was having a real hard time not asking you about that article in the *Times* last week."

"You saw it?"

"Of course I did. It was the *New York Times*. Everyone saw it."

Of course. Everyone. Even out here. The lovely Daphne had already proven that. Thinking of her watching him through the windshield of his Jeep, her eyes so damning, made his skin tight.

He bristled in reaction to the unbidden thought of her. It had been a long time since his thoughts had been so caught up in a woman. Especially to one who so clearly hated him and who he was never going to see again.

"Why don't you just tell them," Mom suggested. "Explain—"

"There's nothing to explain," he said, walking again, trying to shake the remembered sensation of Daphne's eyes judging him.

"Jonah—"

"There is nothing to explain," he repeated, enunciating clearly so she'd get the idea that the conversation was over.

"Well, if you won't stay for me," she said, "if you won't stay in order to get to know your own father—"

He rolled his eyes at her and she smacked his arm. "I am your mother, Jonah. You will not roll your eyes at me."

"Sorry, Mom," he said, truly abashed.

"Like I was saying, if you won't stay for me, or to get to know these truly wonderful men—these kind and generous and complicated men who are your family—at least stay until that Dirty Developer thing blows over."

Ah, his mom. So smart.

He sighed. "If you are asking me, I will stay."

"I know, but I get tired of asking."

"You never ask," he cried, laughing. "I have more money than I know what to do with and you refuse a penny. I try to take you on trips. I tried to buy you that new car—"

"My car is fine."

"Your car is a mess!"

"I don't need your money, or your trips or cars."

"Clearly."

"I need you. Here. For two weeks."

He felt himself strain and push against that promise he'd made. He'd never guessed, being so young and so suddenly on top of the world, that his mother would ever ask for something he didn't want to give. The one thing, actually, that he didn't want to give her.

"Were you unhappy?" he asked, blurting out the question that had been churning in his brain since he saw her smile at Max and Gabe. "All those years with me…did you wish we were with them?"

Tears filled her eyes, turning them to black pools. He was sorry that he made her cry. He was always sorry for that. But it hurt to think that he was second best all these years.

"I wanted to be with you," she said fiercely. "Wherever you were that's where I wanted to be."

He smiled at her. He knew a hedge when he heard one. A half-truth. She'd asked him once if he wanted to know his father and he'd said no. Absolutely no.

At the time his six-year-old brain thought it might mean sharing his mother. And he hated that.

His thirty-year-old brain wasn't all that different. But he did recognize what he did to her when he'd told her no. The wall he'd built. He made it impossible to try to have both— her husband and sons all together.

Of course those letters Patrick had written telling Iris he didn't want her, those letters put up quite a wall, too. Jonah didn't like the idea of her here chasing after the man who'd rejected her. Hurt her so much. There was far too much potential for more pain for his mother here.

"Mom, why do you want this so bad?" he asked. "The guy told you no."

"And then he said yes." Iris shrugged. "We both made mistakes."

It was a terrible answer, in Jonah's book. Patrick changing his mind about having Iris come back didn't erase the thirty years that his mom missed the man.

She'd pretended she didn't, but Jonah wasn't blind.

And it made him very nervous. Mom was walking toward a freight train of pain and he needed to pull her out of the way.

"If I don't stay, if I say no, will you go back home?" he asked.

She shook her head.

"Will you come to New York for a visit?" he asked.

And his mom, who knew him so well, shook her head again. "I want to get to know these men," she said. "I'll stay for a while."

There was a buzzing in the back of his head, a sense of impending doom.

"Mom," he whispered, wishing so badly she didn't feel anything for Patrick.

"I know," she said, holding up her hand. "But I wouldn't change it if I could."

He would, he thought. He'd change everything about the damn situation if he could.

Well, crap. He was going to have to stay. Maybe he could derail the freight train.

Daphne's green eyes were there in his head and he slid his sunglasses back on. Perhaps he would be seeing her again.

"I'm at the Athens Motel tonight," he said. "I'll check into the Riverview tomorrow morning." He saw her relax. Melt a little, as though whatever pins had been keeping her shoulders up around her ears, whatever stress was making her lips tense, her fingers clench slowly faded away.

He kissed her lightly on the forehead.

Love, he thought, was just a disaster waiting to happen.

DAPHNE TOED OFF her mucky galoshes and stepped into her kitchen in her bare feet. The rainy spring had done wonders for her asparagus and between that and her trouble finding reliable delivery guys, her mornings were insane. She woke up at dawn and ran a marathon by 8:00 a.m. Luckily her mother, Gloria, had been coming over in the mornings to help Helen get ready for school.

"Hi, Helen," Daphne said, tugging her daughter's long ponytail and taking in her ensemble. Helen's fashion sense this morning involved the top of a genie costume that she'd worn in a school musical two years ago. It was pink, sparkly and showed about an inch of her little girl's belly.

Damn teen pop stars and MTV and hormones in meat and milk or whatever was making little girls grow up way too fast these days.

"You're not wearing that to school," she said, point-blank.

"Mom." Helen groaned.

"Sorry, kiddo. Go on up and change."

Helen cast one more pleading gaze at her grandmother, who only laughed. "I told you, you wouldn't get away with it," Gloria said. Helen flounced up the stairs, the spangles on her shirt twitching and twirling.

"I swear she's seven going on seventeen." Daphne sighed, taking the mug of coffee her mother slid across the counter at her.

"It's not much different than when you were a kid," Gloria said, arching one dark eyebrow. Daphne did not take after her petite, dark-haired Italian mother, despite how much she wished she had. Instead, she was the spitting image of her lying, cheating, Swedish father. Blond hair, broad shoulders and a fierce temper. She was a genetic delight. "The clothes are just smaller."

Daphne smiled and tried to drink as much caffeine as she was capable in the few minutes she had before driving Helen to school. Mornings were still chilly these days and she warmed her palms around the Del Monte seed mug.

"She asked for two sandwiches in her lunch again today," Gloria said and Daphne frowned.

"Didn't she have breakfast?" she asked. Helen's appetite usually hovered around birdlike, except for the occasional growth spurts in which case her appetite approached don't-get-in-my-way territory.

Gloria nodded. "She ate all her yogurt. But that's every day this week she's asked for an extra something."

Strange. Daphne checked her watch. She'd have to ask Helen about it on the road.

"Helen is also turning into a gossip columnist," Gloria said, wiping off the last of the breakfast dishes and setting them back in the oak cabinet.

Daphne nearly choked on her coffee. "I wonder where she gets it?" She cast a look at her mother who, as the resident gossip queen, had given up amateur status and gone pro a few years ago. Gloria took "news" very seriously.

"Very funny. But she's all wound up over what's happening down at the Riverview. Thanks to her friend Josie, she's an expert on Patrick's youngest."

"Jonah," Daphne said, trying to hide behind her coffee cup, so her mother wouldn't pick up the blushes she couldn't control. Mom was like a drug-sniffing dog when it came to those sorts of things. She could take a wayward glance or a blush and turn it into a torrid love affair in less time than it took Helen to change her clothes.

"Sounds like quite a guy." Gloria pretended to be nonchalant but "why don't you marry him and give me more grandbabies" was written all over her. She did this whenever a young man got within dating distance.

"That's one way of putting it," Daphne hedged. Utterly inappropriate or a low-down scumbag were a couple of others. She checked her watch. "Helen! Let's go, slowpoke!" she shouted, wanting to flee the kitchen before her mother started into her biannual monologue about men, ticking clocks and loneliness.

A real laugh riot, that monologue.

"Sweetheart?" Gloria said. Daphne groaned and just laid her head on the counter, like a woman at the guillotine. "Would it kill you to date?"

"Yes," she said into the yellow Formica. "It would kill me."

"I'm being serious," Gloria insisted, pulling Daphne up by the back of her shirt. "This Jonah fellow is a young man, single, apparently attractive—"

"And leaving, Mom. He's not sticking around. He's probably already gone. Which wouldn't matter because he's the last person in the world I would date."

"Apparently every man within a thirty-mile radius shares that status."

"Mom—"

"You didn't even fight for Gabe Mitchell!"

Daphne rolled her eyes. Her mother could not let go of the brief relationship she had with Gabe. "There was nothing to fight for, Mom. The man was in love with his ex-wife. What was I supposed to do?"

Gloria's face became a mix of pity and pleading and

Daphne hated it. "You're too young to spend your life covered in mud. You used to be so carefree and spontaneous. You used to be fun."

"I'm still fun, ask Helen."

"Grown-up fun. Sex fun."

Daphne groaned and held up her hand. "I am too busy to date. I am too busy for—" she dropped her voice, uncomfortable even saying the word "—sex fun. I am raising Helen and trying to expand my business—"

"Excuses," Gloria interrupted, her eyes flashing, her short brown hair practically bristling. Gloria had finally found love again with a high school English teacher who lived twenty miles away. They dated, went to movies, traveled. They weren't married, didn't live together and the relationship was, for Gloria, perfect.

And that perfection gave her a license to harangue Daphne on the subject of second chances on a regular basis. "You're too scared to even try."

A charged stillness filled Daphne, like the air before a lightning strike. Her mother was right. She was scared. Scared of being hurt. Of being rejected. Of being left behind all over again.

"You are so beautiful and strong. Any man would be lucky to have you." Her mother's soft voice was tempting, but reality was reality and that's where Daphne parked her butt these days.

"You're my mother, you are supposed to say that." Daphne brushed crumbs from the counter into her hands, looking anywhere but at her mother. "But my track record speaks for itself."

"What does that mean?"

"It means—" she swallowed, the words wedged behind

her pride and reluctant to come out "—men don't want me. Not permanently." She dumped the crumbs in the garbage by the sink, wishing she could do the same with this conversation.

"Oh my God!" Gloria cried, spinning Daphne around. "How can you say that?"

"Well, for one, Dad—"

"Your father wasn't cut out to be a father. His leaving had nothing to do with you."

"I was seven, Mom. I went to bed and had a father but when I woke up he was gone. Trust me, that feels pretty personal. And Jake pretty much confirms it."

Gloria sighed. "Well, you barely gave Jake a chance to be a father. Or a husband."

"Jake wanted to leave," Daphne insisted. "You think I pushed him out the door, but trust me, he doesn't see it that way. I gave Jake his freedom."

They heard Helen's footsteps upstairs, a signal to stop before she heard them.

"Not every man leaves," Gloria said.

"You're right," Daphne agreed. "Just the ones I love."

Helen tromped in wearing a far more appropriate red T-shirt with a big yellow flower on the front, looking like the quirky funny seven-year-old she was, rather than a young hooker in training. "Mom, everybody in school wears shirts like that," she said, grabbing her bulging book bag and brown bag lunch.

"Everyone but you, Helen," Daphne said sweetly, ushering her out the door toward the truck. "Everyone but you."

They drove down the driveway toward the road into town and Daphne unrolled her window, the morning finally warming up. The breeze, warm and smelling like pine and manure from Sven's farm, curled through the cab.

The For Sale sign was still posted and she hadn't heard a word about her offer. She stuck her tongue out at the ramshackle old house as they drove by just to make herself feel better.

"Hey, Mom, guess what I heard?" Helen asked, turning bright eyes to Daphne. Her still chubby cheeks were pink and the wind teased hair loose from her braid to whip it around her face. Daphne smiled, loving her daughter so much sometimes it was like a physical pain. Budding gossip columnist or no.

"What did you hear?" she asked like a woman on the edge of her seat. She shouldn't encourage this or Helen would turn out worse than Mom, but she was too darn cute not to.

"Josie said Jonah moved into the inn and Josie was trying to spy on him but her mom caught her and made her do dishes with Chef Tim."

"Jonah moved into the inn?" Now Daphne really was on the edge of her seat.

"That's what Josie said yesterday on the playground."

"When did he move in?"

"Yesterday morning. Josie said she watched him unpack his bags and talk on the phone. She said he talks on the phone a lot."

"How long is he staying?" Daphne asked and wished she didn't care. She wished her cheeks weren't hot at the mention of his name. Wished she could stop interrogating her seven-year-old as if she were the sole witness to a crime.

"I don't know," Helen said. "I'll ask Josie."

Daphne told herself that she was just curious about a

man so utterly different from her. Still, she had to bite
back a long list of questions she had about the man.

When is he leaving?

Why is he such a jerk?

Why does he look so good in blue jeans?

Is he married?

"You want me to ask if he's married?" Helen asked and
Daphne nearly drove off the side of the road.

"What?" *Good God? Am I talking out loud?* "Why?"

"So, you can date. Josie said he's really cute." Helen
waggled her eyebrows, something Daphne did as a joke
and it was about a million times funnier on her seven-year-
old daughter.

"Have you been talking to Grandma?" Daphne demanded.

"No," Helen said. "I told you I was talking to Josie and
she can totally find out if he's married."

"Even if he was single, I'm not going to be dating him,"
Daphne told her daughter in all seriousness, hoping to end
this conversation.

Helen harrumphed and looked out the window, pulling
blond hair out of her eyes. Daphne had known that the little
cocoon of Athens Organics, the country she'd created of
Daphne and Helen, wouldn't last forever. Helen was bound
to get interested in things outside of the farm and her
mother, but Daphne had never really suspected it would be
her love life.

"Is it because Daddy's back?" Helen asked. "Is that
why you don't date anyone?"

Oh God, Daphne had feared this would happen when
Jake came back around. She'd suspected Helen would get
her hopes up and start thinking that they'd be a family
again. The divorce wasn't so hard the first time around—

Helen had been so young. But this time, when Jake left—and he would, he was a leaver—his absence would ruin a seven-year-old's high hopes and fantasies.

"Honey, Dad and I aren't getting back together," Daphne said clearly. She decided to slow down, deliveries be damned, and pull over to the side of the road so she and Helen could really talk. "We're just friends and we're going to all these parties to help him with his new job." She put the truck in Park and let it idle.

"I know," Helen said, and Daphne wondered if she was just saying what Daphne wanted to hear. "But it would be nice if we were all friends. And I think Daddy loves you."

"No, honey, he doesn't." She stroked her daughter's cornsilk hair. He never really had. Not the real her. And certainly not enough to make it work. "But he loves you like crazy," she said, smiling and tugging on Helen's ponytail. Soon Helen would want to cut off that long hair, wear something cooler than a long braid like her mommy. Daphne dreaded the day.

Helen smiled, some of the seriousness leeching from her face, only to be replaced by the quicksilver joy of a seven-year-old. "He's taking me to the drive-in tonight. A double feature."

Daphne steered the truck back onto the road. It was Friday and Jake's night with Helen. She'd convinced herself at some point in the past eight months that this one night a week Jake had with his daughter was a blessing for all of them. He got to know his daughter. Helen got to know her father in a very small way. A small, very regulated way that would hopefully keep her protected when he reverted to his leaving ways. And during those few hours Daphne got some work done.

On Friday nights.

When the rest of the world was dating or watching movies as families or fighting or making love or putting their children to bed. She was walking asparagus fields.

It didn't feel like a blessing.

It felt lonely.

She dropped Helen off at school, glad her little girl wasn't too old or too concerned about being cool to forgo the kiss goodbye.

And only when she was halfway to her first delivery did she realize she never asked why Helen needed extra food in her lunch.

CHAPTER FOUR

THE RIVERVIEW INN had wireless Internet, Jonah could get a cell phone signal, his mother had been bringing him coffee and food. So despite having been forced to stay, he was doing a very good job of not leaving his cabin.

Jonah had been at the inn for exactly twenty-nine hours and he'd managed to avoid seeing anyone but his mother. It helped that he was busy. At least it gave him an excuse for his mother when she tried to persuade him to join her for a walk.

"We passed the second soil testing with flying colors," Gary told him. "We've got the green light to keep building."

"Excellent news," Jonah said, though he had not expected anything less. "We're ahead of schedule. I'll contact Herb and we'll get crews in there next week."

"Okay, but do you want to do anything with the news-papers?"

"Send the press release like you always do," he said, jotting "call Herb" on the pad at his elbow.

"But those press releases don't go anywhere. We never follow up and maybe with this bad press we've been getting—"

"No explanations, Gary."

"I'm not saying we explain. I'm saying we clear the air.

We tell the world what we're doing and maybe get some wheels greased for Haven House."

"The world isn't going to help us with Haven House."

"Donations would help and a little good press would make me sleep easier."

"We don't need good press, so why pander?"

"You are the most stubborn man I've ever met, Jonah. I'm your partner. And I'm telling you—I'm actually saying it loud and clear so you understand—you're making a mistake. We need to talk to the papers. I know at least four journalists who would love to interview us."

Ouch. He and Gary didn't often disagree but when they did, it had been proven time and time again that Gary was right.

Jonah liked to pretend that wasn't the case, but facts didn't lie.

"Fine. They can interview you."

"I'm not the Dirty Developer," Gary said. "I'm the Dirty Developer's associate."

Jonah knew it was practically a done deal before he even agreed. Gary was tricky that way. Tricky and smart. "Fine. Get in touch with them and e-mail me the details."

Jonah glanced at the window and saw the little girl duck again, just out of sight. The bushes rustled and he heard her whispering to someone or into a tape recorder. The redhead—Jonah would guess she was about ten—had been out there for most of the day, spying on him. The spy had astounding stamina and determination. He'd only been working and even he was beginning to find that dull.

He smiled, remembering doing a similar thing to Sheila after finding out she was a full-blooded Hopi Indian. He'd followed her hoping to see some scalping.

But she only grocery shopped and walked her dog. The disappointment had been sharp so he decided to give young Mata Hari a thrill.

"Gary," he said, watching the window from the corner of his eye. "Listen carefully. We're going to put the bodies—"

"Bodies?"

"Right. The dead bodies. The dead bodies we killed." He winced at his redundancy but the bushes were unnaturally silent. "We're going to put them in the river."

Something fell outside his window. A bush rustled and the little girl yelped.

"No mistakes," Jonah said, smiling, straining to try to see the girl. "Or I'll kill you, too."

"Jonah, you should come back to the city," Gary said. "All that clear air is making you crazy."

Jonah heard the little girl talking to someone then heard the deep rumble of Patrick's voice and his smile vanished. "Send me that e-mail," Jonah said, distracted by the sound of Patrick and the girl walking up the sidewalk outside his cottage.

Great. Visitors.

"Got it," Gary answered and hung up as a knock sounded at the door.

Jonah opened the door and found the old man, his hand on the girl's shoulder.

The little girl, wearing head to toe purple, looked tortured, but she still managed to give him the evil eye. He swallowed a crack of laughter.

"This is Josie," Patrick said, his gaze flicking between them. "And she has something to say."

Jonah wanted to roll his eyes, call out the old man for this useless display of what…manners? Honor? Jonah didn't believe a moment of it. Patrick wouldn't know honor if it had bitten him on the ass.

"I've been spying on you," Josie said, gesturing limply to the window.

"And…?" Patrick prompted.

"And—" she rolled her eyes "—I'm sorry."

Jonah nodded at her and her tortured expression changed slightly. She craned her neck to get a better look inside his cabin.

The girl was stubborn, and Jonah understood stubborn. *My kind of kid,* he thought.

"You go see what Chef Tim has for you to do in the kitchen," Patrick told the girl and she scowled.

"Again?"

"You got caught," Patrick said, shaking his head, "again."

"But—" She looked at Jonah then Patrick, and Jonah realized that she didn't want to leave the old man alone with him, maybe suspecting Jonah would add Patrick to the pile of bodies in the river.

"I knew you were out there," he told the little girl. "I made that up about the bodies."

"Really?" she asked, eyeing him shrewdly and again he almost laughed.

"Really."

He felt Patrick's gaze on him, hopeful and surprised. *Yes,* Jonah wanted to snap at him, *the Dirty Developer has a sense of humor.*

But he didn't want Patrick to know anything about him.

She hesitated as if to say she didn't believe him but then she nodded. "Okay. But if Patrick goes missing, I'm an eyewitness. I'll testify."

Jonah blinked, stunned slightly by the legal vernacular.

"Get going," Patrick said, bodily turning the girl around and giving her a push toward the lodge.

Josie sighed heavily and stomped off, leaving Patrick and Jonah alone. Jonah realized this was the moment Patrick had been waiting for since he'd arrived.

Josie hadn't been the only one haunting the outside of his cabin.

"Josie and her mother were in a scrape with the law last winter," Patrick explained. "She saw and heard some things she shouldn't have and spent some time in court this spring testifying. She caught on to the lingo."

Jonah watched the girl go until the door of the lodge shut behind her.

"Why don't you come on out?" Patrick said. "I'll give you a tour. Take you down to the river." His tone seemed casual, but he couldn't control the hope that rolled off him, nearly suffocating Jonah.

"I'm working."

Patrick sucked in a quick breath but kept his smile intact. The man wasn't going to budge.

"Your mother—"

"Don't try to use my mother to get me to do what you want me to do," he said. "It won't work. In fact, it will make me like you less. Not that it's possible."

Jonah tried to shut the door but Patrick got his hand in there before he could. Jonah was stunned briefly by the sudden sharpness in the old man's eyes, the sudden anger.

"I didn't know about you," Patrick said. "Your mother never told me. If I had known, I would have done anything to get you back."

Jonah knew that, of course. His mother had made very

sure that he understood that Patrick had not rejected Jonah. He'd only rejected his wife. Banished her from her own family.

"Is that supposed to make me forgive you?" Jonah asked.

"I don't understand what you are angry with me for." Patrick truly looked lost. Clueless and that told him even further what Iris meant to this man.

"I'm angry," he said clearly, making sure nothing would get misunderstood or forgotten, "because you never signed those divorce papers. You kept her chained to you for thirty years like she didn't matter. You broke my mother's heart. I'm angry because I grew up with a mother who every day tried to hide the fact that she was unhappy." Patrick's face crumpled, his fire extinguished. "And, no, there is nothing you can do to make me forgive that."

With that, before the old man could say anything more, Jonah shut the door in his face.

PATRICK STARED at the closed door.

Heartsick, he battled nausea and chest pains. Confusion and grief made his head fuzzy and light.

What am I supposed to do?

He watched Max walk out of the lodge into the woods and thought about calling out to him. Trying to talk to him about this mess with Jonah. But his boys weren't invested. They wanted him to protect himself, not get involved. Gabe in particular wanted him to let it go.

Even Max, last night, had said if Jonah wasn't interested in bridging the gaps then maybe it wasn't meant to be.

Patrick couldn't believe that this family wasn't meant to be.

Against all odds, Jonah was here. In cabin five.

Patrick simply needed to figure out how to get Jonah out of cabin five.

He knew that if he asked Iris to help him, to force the boy's hand since he'd do anything for his mother, some of this heartache would be avoided.

But Patrick didn't want her help. He wanted to feed the small fire of his grudge against her.

What she'd done was unforgivable. Despite the fact that he understood the whys and the reasons, he couldn't forgive her.

She'd left them, him and the boys. Walked away in the middle of the night thirty years ago and had stayed away for three months before writing Patrick a letter asking to come home. He'd told her no. He'd been angry. Spiteful and hurt and he had no way of knowing that she was pregnant and her terrifying erratic behavior before she left had been caused by depression brought on by the pregnancy.

She wrote again, nine months later when Jonah must have been a few months old. By that time Patrick had his life in a rhythm. Something that worked. It wasn't perfect and often it wasn't pretty, but he was raising his boys and he'd decided that life was easier without her.

He'd been wrong, of course.

When he'd sent those letters to her, telling her not to come, that they were doing fine without her, he'd been thinking of himself and the boys.

He'd been thinking about Iris's depression and the way it could make his life terrifying.

Happiness—hers, his, the boys—he hadn't thought of. Now he wished he had. Staring at the door of cabin five and knowing his son was in there, blaming Patrick for things that weren't all his fault, he wished he could have seen the future. In order to prevent this itchy heartache in his chest, he wouldn't have kept his wife away.

He could have had his son.

Like a magnet, he found himself pulled in the direction of Iris. He wanted to remind her of the mistakes she'd made, the mess she'd made of their lives—the years they'd wasted.

It was, after all, her fault.

He'd been trying to keep his distance from her since her return a few weeks ago. He liked to pretend that he didn't know this woman who looked like an older, sadder version of the woman he'd fallen in love with on a vacation to the Jersey Shore. He wanted to pretend that the years and the betrayal had changed their core.

Now, however, he walked to the gazebo where he knew she'd be.

And there she was. Bouncing, loving and generally hogging baby Stella as she had since her arrival.

Their first grandchild. The thought caught him in the throat and he couldn't breathe. He just watched Iris with Stella and ached.

It was a milestone they should have celebrated together—arm in arm, in love, proud and happy.

She robbed him of that.

She didn't hear him approach, thank God, all of her energy focused on the pink bundle in her arms.

A tiny hand came up out of the blanket and patted Iris's mouth, reaching for the dangling earrings she wore.

"Pretty soon, Stella," she cooed, touching her nose to the baby's. "Pretty soon you'll have your hands on everything."

The hot mix of emotions built in him, filling his chest and his head. He couldn't make sense of them. Couldn't put a name to everything that made him want to grab her and shake her. Touch her.

Oh God, how could he want to touch her so bad when she'd lied to him? Kept his son from him? Why did he want to hold her and ease the pain he saw in the weary set of her shoulders, the bowed curve of her neck as if the whole world was pressing on her?

It didn't make sense. But anger made sense. Anger worked. So he concentrated on that.

He started to put words together, hurtful words telling her exactly what she'd done to him.

"Patrick," she said, interrupting his mental tirade, not even turning to look at him. "I was wondering when you'd come looking for me. Things aren't going well with Jonah?"

He shook his head, the mix of emotions making words impossible. *I'm mad,* he wanted to howl.

"You want to take that out on me?" she asked. "Yell at me? Make me feel worse than I already do?"

Yes!

Finally she looked at him, her black eyes a well of hurt. Of regret. But she would let him do it. She would let him yell and rage and blame her for all the misery at the inn. But it wouldn't add to the pain in her eyes. The burden she carried on those strong, elegant shoulders.

I can't make her feel worse than she does, he realized.

"No," he whispered. He shook his head, weary suddenly as the emotions that had fueled him dissipated like fog in the sun.

Stella fussed, a little cry that turned Iris's attention to the little girl. "Hello, there. Hello, little love," she whispered and he felt that bit of nonsense, that soft breath of air from his wife's mouth enter his tortured self and calm him down.

He and Stella both stopped fussing.

"She's a lot like Max was as a baby," Iris said, with the familiar ribbon of the Hudson River behind her. A careful truce was offered in her eyes, the merest hint of a question. *Will you let it go?* her eyes asked. *Please, for both of us, let it go.* "He didn't like sleeping, either. Wanted to be in the middle of the action all the time."

Patrick felt the memories creep through him. Images of the boys' early years when they were a family—memories he'd sequestered and quarantined.

I can't do this. I can't pretend everything is okay. I can't.

But he wanted to.

"Remember?" she asked.

Don't make me let go of my resentment.

"He was a busy guy," he said, giving in, knowing it was a useless battle. He let the memories out. The happiness of those days. The peace and kindness whirled through him. "I thought he'd never sleep through the night."

"Unlike Gabe," she said. "He slept through his first six months."

"Six months? More like six years." Patrick smiled at the memories.

"Slept and ate, that's about it. Remember when we went camping that summer?"

Patrick laughed, knowing exactly what she was thinking of, the incident conjured up by her voice as if it had happened yesterday. "He slept through that big storm."

"Not just the storm," she said, swaying slightly when Stella began to fuss. "He slept through the tent collapsing and all of us running around trying to fix it."

Iris brushed her fingers over the little girl's face and Patrick could feel that touch as if it were his flesh Iris stroked. These feelings entered with the memories, unwanted hangers-on.

"I pulled in as much of the tent as I could and ended up balling up the rest and sleeping on it." Patrick cleared his throat and stared at his hands. "One of the worst nights of sleep I ever had. I was sore for months."

"Remember in the morning, Gabe woke us up to tell us the tent fell down. Like we didn't know." Iris laughed. "Oh my Lord, that boy could sleep through anything. Jonah was the same way."

At the mention of their youngest son's name, the air between them changed. Became heavier, darker.

"He's not talking to me," Patrick murmured. "He won't even come out of the cabin."

"Jonah doesn't want to be here," Iris told him what he already knew. "And he can be very stubborn."

"What do I do?" Patrick asked, sitting in one of the wrought-iron chairs. His bones felt sore, taxed to their limit just by holding him up.

"You be patient with him," Iris said. "He's stubborn but his heart is so good."

"The Dirty Developer?" Patrick asked, the name tasting gross on his tongue.

"If I explained his business to you, he would never forgive me," she said. He glanced at her and he could see her strength. Hard-won in Arizona, raising a boy without him. She was like bedrock and she wasn't going to budge on this.

Admiration—one more thing he didn't want to feel for her—seeped into the mysterious whirl of feelings he was trying to ignore.

A breeze came up from the Hudson and sent her earrings into motion and Stella reached again for the silver. "But you have to trust me—"

He laughed. He laughed before he could help it. He was sore and raw and he did trust Iris. He could see what the years had done to her, the regret she lived with.

But he laughed because he hurt so much and he wanted her to hurt a little, too. It was cruel. And sick.

"I'm sorry." He knew his baffled heart showed in his eyes. "It's just hard."

"Trusting me?" she asked quietly.

"You walked away from me and I know you were sick, but—" He took a deep breath. "It's easier to hate you."

"It's easier to hate you, too," she said and his head snapped toward her. "You told me you didn't want me. You rejected me. Twice. Do you think it's easy for me to swallow my pride and be here now?"

He hadn't thought of that.

"No," he said. "I don't suppose it is."

"He was sick," she said and his body went on alert. He had told Iris he didn't want to know anything about Jonah, that he wanted to learn everything on his own. But his methods weren't working and he was thirsty for information, for details about his son. "For so long. Pneumonia and asthma and fevers. We thought the chicken pox was going to kill him. But he was so tough." She smiled, looking at the baby.

I should have been there, he wanted to scream, his anger and resentment surging like high tide. *You should have told me. I should have known. I would have helped. I would have sat by his bed with you. I would have worried and cried and—*

"Jonah would kill me for telling you this, but you have

to understand where he's coming from," Iris said, staring at the river. "Jonah was always an outsider. He was too small and too sick most of the time to play outside with other kids. And just when he'd get better, something else would happen and he'd be back in the hospital or on bed rest. So, he didn't have many friends. He had me and he had Sheila. When he was little I used to hear him playing in his room and he would pretend that he was in the Boy Scouts or at summer camp. He would make up stories about his father and his six brothers." She held the baby tighter as the breeze from the river blew through the gazebo. "He'd pretend you were all lumberjacks. Or policemen. Or firefighters. Something strong and big. Manly." She glanced at him over her shoulder. "You don't have to be a psychologist to understand why."

Patrick shook his head. Nope. He didn't. And his heart broke for that little boy, so alone and sick.

"He found the letters you sent," she said. "We had a tiny apartment and I thought I'd hid them carefully but when he was getting over the chicken pox, he found them. And everything changed." She shook her head. "After that illness he wasn't sick like that anymore. He got stronger. He got healthier and as he got older he seemed to want to protect me. And that's why he's here."

"Protecting you from what?"

"You, Patrick. He's protecting me from getting hurt again by you."

The breeze was suddenly too cold and he felt every year he'd spent alone like a wall crushing him.

She sat beside him, not touching him, but close enough that his skin could feel hers. He could smell the spicy, sweet scent of her perfume and it made him dizzy.

"What are we going to do?" he asked, staring at the river.

Touch her. Hold her. Make it better.

Oh God, he wanted to. He wanted to be comforted. And he wanted to comfort her, even while he was the one hurting her.

"Well," she whispered, lifting Stella away from her chest and handing him to her. "I'll tell you what I do. I come out here every day and I hold this little girl."

Patrick's arms accepted the precious weight of his grandchild and the heaviness lifted momentarily from his chest.

"And I forget about the past," Iris told him. Her hand brushed his shoulder, a fingertip grazing the flesh of his neck. His whole body flooded with blood and sensation.

He concentrated on Stella and waited for the feelings to recede. It took a while, considering how long he'd been ignoring such things. Iris sat beside him, gazing out at the water and the land, breathing deeply of the air and sighing as if everything she wanted was right here. Despite the pain. Despite the past.

She sat as though there was nothing else to want in the whole world.

CHAPTER FIVE

JONAH STOPPED running and stared at the For Sale sign nailed on the broken wooden fence. Wiping the sweat from his eyes he climbed the small embankment beside the gravel road and peered over the overgrown hedge at what was for sale.

Land. Lots of it.

A giant farmhouse with three outbuildings, one of them falling apart.

His heart, pounding hard thanks to his six-minute miles, pounded harder.

Few people knew it and no one really would believe it, but Jonah put a lot of stock in signs. Signs from God, signs from the planet, signs from his better sense.

And land for sale so close to the Riverview, but with a better view and fewer trees and better drainage, land so perfect he'd be a fool not to make an offer…if that wasn't a sign, what was?

He jumped down onto the gravel road and unzipped the small sport sack that his mother made him promise to wear around his waist when he went running.

"You're asthmatic, Jonah," she'd said. "If you're going to be stupid and run, don't be stupid and dead."

It was a good point and so, in his pack he had his inhaler, his cell phone and twenty bucks.

Just in case.

He hit speed dial and got Gary's voice mail.

"Gary," he said, "I need you to contact a Sven Lungren about some land he has for sale up here." He read off the number on the sign and turned to assess the view of the mountains and the Hudson Valley.

Perfect.

"It's a great spot for a hotel," he said. "Something good for families." He thought of everything the Riverview wasn't. All the ways he could compete with and crush the Mitchells. "Maybe a waterslide. A state-of-the-art spa. Think big."

He disconnected his call and dropped the phone in the slim pack.

Guilt was a foreign emotion and he plucked it out of the mix of things he was feeling and tossed it away. He owed the Mitchells nothing, less than nothing. And should he build a hotel here, something bigger and better than what his brothers had, then that was just the nature of business.

Darwin, as Gary so often said, was really a capitalist. And if it gave Jonah a personal thrill to imagine Patrick's face when Jonah broke ground up here, well, then, that was icing on the cake.

A cramp zinged up his calf and he winced, grabbing a hold of the fence and stretching it out. Suddenly he was all too aware of how tired he was. How all of his muscles were feeling shaky.

Glancing at his watch, he realized he'd been running for an hour.

Day two at the inn and this morning he'd been tired of his cabin and adamant about not making nice with the Mitchells so he'd gone out for exercise and now was faced with an hour-long run back.

He could call his mother to pick him up, but he hadn't indulged in that kind of behavior since Joe Meyers kicked his ass in grade school.

"Hey," a small voice behind him said and he whirled, coming face-to-face with a miniature Daphne Larson. A woman he knew he shouldn't remember in such complete detail, down to her lush upper lip and the smudge of mud across her forehead.

But he did.

Foolish, really. But there it was—the woman was stuck in his brain. Probably another damn sign, this one not so good.

This little girl had the same white-blond hair, same grass-green eyes. But her mouth was purple and something sticky and purple was smeared across her cheek.

And this little girl was smiling at him, which he was very sure Daphne wouldn't do. Ever.

"Hey yourself," he said, wiping sweat off his forehead with the sleeve of his shirt.

"You lost?"

He made a point of looking around. "Nope. You?"

She laughed. "I live over there." She jerked her thumb behind her.

"Is your mom Daphne?" he asked, the resemblance too striking for her to be anyone else.

She nodded and lifted a bare purple-stained Popsicle stick to her mouth. Chewing on it, she eyed him sideways.

"You're Jonah, aren't you?" she finally asked and he blinked at her.

"How do you know my name?"

"Josie is, like, my best friend and she told me yesterday."

Josie. The young spy.

"And you look like Patrick," she continued. "He is your dad, right?"

Just like that the sweat running down his back went cold. They didn't look alike at all really. The same eyes, but lots of people had blue eyes.

"Helen?" someone yelled, saving him from having to explain the difference between sperm donors and fathers. He doubted Daphne of the lush mouth and stalwart ideas would appreciate that talk coming from the Dirty Developer.

"Over here, Mom!" Helen yelled over her shoulder.

He braced himself for what was about to happen. Daphne would come out of the brush, flushed maybe, something green in her hair. And she'd be angry, no doubt, to find him contaminating her daughter by standing within a five-foot radius of her.

Runner's high, finding that land for sale, the little girl, so cute and so like her mother, all made him suddenly eager to see Daphne again. To see if she was what he remembered.

"Helen, how many times have I told you—"

And, there she was, just as he'd imagined, including the green stuff in her hair. And she was everything he remembered.

In a word, lovely.

"Oh," she said, pausing briefly when she saw him. Then she moved to stand between him and Helen, defending her girl against him.

That stung a little, that she thought so little of him. But really, what did he expect? She thought he was the Dirty Developer.

Don't explain. Don't beg. Don't apologize.

Sometimes his mantra got in the way of getting dates.

"What are you doing here?" she asked.

"Running," he said.

"From the inn?" Daphne asked. "That's miles away."

Her wide green eyes slid down his body, taking in his shorts and the sweat-soaked Late Night with David Lettermen T-shirt. Her cheeks, tanned from the sun, turned pink as though she had some kind of opinion on what she saw, a slightly inappropriate opinion. Suddenly the sweat was back.

Hot this time.

He lifted the hem of his shirt and wiped his forehead, revealing a good few inches of his stomach and he practically felt the rush of air she sucked in.

He fought back a smile. She might not like what she thought he did, but she didn't mind looking at him.

"Do you…ah…need…a towel or…something?" she asked, and he dropped his shirt.

"A glass of water would be great."

She nodded, turned slightly and paused. He realized she didn't know whether or not to invite him into her home. And he knew her hesitation wasn't because of the sweat.

"I'll wait out here," he said, unsmiling as the old war waged in him.

Just tell her. Explain that the papers got it wrong, that he was actually the opposite of what she thought. He was one of the good guys. He was actually a lot like her.

He wondered if the explanation would change what she thought about him. If she'd look at him differently.

But what would be the point, really? In the end, her opinion of him, good or bad, was inconsequential. It didn't change his work. His life. That was true for everyone's opinion.

It was the lesson he'd learned over and over—beaten into him by bullies and business. The only thing that mattered was the work. His work spoke for itself and he didn't need anyone to tell him he did a good job.

Wavering on his conviction because he was attracted to a blonde would be the height of pointlessness. There were lots of blondes. Maybe not as interesting as this one, but still plenty to be had.

Besides, Daphne was probably married, despite the lack of a ring on her finger. Women like her, with daughters like Helen, were the kind men held on to.

Though, he thought, glancing at the land for sale, they might be neighbors. He should at least try to be nice.

"Don't be ridiculous," she said, smiling, though it was not the most sincere effort he'd seen. She had good manners that insisted she allow the Dirty Developer onto her organic farm.

Helen tugged on Daphne's sweater.

"Sorry." Daphne grinned with half her mouth, a shy abashed sort of smile and something pinged in his chest. A sharp cord of attraction. "This is my daughter, Helen. Helen, this is Jonah Mit—"

"Closky," he corrected, more harshly than he needed to, but everyone was getting just a little too cozy with his bloodlines.

"Right," Daphne said, that abashed smile gone. "Jonah Closky. Come on then." She walked past the place in the bushes she'd climbed out of, to the proper driveway, complete with the white picket fence and the sun-dappled trees.

A white farmhouse with black shutters and a mess of plants and chairs and kid stuff on the porch, sat smack dab in the middle of acres of black fields filled with green crops.

Momentarily he worried he was going to have to get his inhaler out.

"Has my mom seen this?" he asked.

"My farm?" Daphne asked over her shoulder, her features adding to the beauty of the place. "I don't think so."

"She would love it here," he said, taking it all in while Helen ran ahead. Daphne paused and watched him.

Nice one, he thought, *why don't you just go ahead and tell her everything about yourself.* "Go figure," he said as if he didn't understand his mother's inclinations.

"Your mother doesn't strike me as a farmer," Daphne said, ignoring his sarcasm.

"Oh?" he asked carefully, every protective instinct in him rising ready to do battle. "What does she strike you as?"

"An artist." Daphne shrugged and Jonah struggled to find the earth under him. It had been her dream—her dream and her secret—that she'd never breathed a word to him. But growing up he'd seen the community college class lists. The pottery classes she'd circled but never signed up for because of time and money. Now, of course, he made sure she had all the opportunity in the world to follow that inclination and, with tears in her eyes, she'd accepted the potter's wheel for Christmas five years ago. And the kiln two years ago.

"She cleaned houses," he said. Blurted it out actually. Not that he was ashamed. He was proud of her. Grateful. In awe of what she'd done in order to keep him in tennis shoes and good schools.

"So did my mom," Daphne said, her expression unreadable.

Common ground, apparently. Now they could have some kind of heartwarming discussion about all those Saturdays they'd played quietly in some stranger's yard while their mothers cleaned toilets until their hands were raw.

"How are things going at the inn?" Daphne asked softly. "I talked to Alice—"

"Fine." Their common ground—not that he wanted it—was obliterated.

"I'm sorry," she said. "I shouldn't pry."

Damn right. "What's that?" he asked, pointing to the field with the most workers in it.

"Vegetables," she said.

"I'm familiar with the idea, but what kind?"

"Asparagus," she said.

"You've got lots of it," he observed.

"A banner year. We're picking practically around the clock. Strawberries are next," she said, and he followed her pointed finger to the grove of apple trees surrounding another green field on the opposite end of her land. The wind shifted and her scent was carried to him on the breeze. The woman smelled like grass. "Next year we're going to try pick-your-own."

"You're going to let strangers onto your land? Near your home?" he asked, horrified. Business was business. No one he worked with, not even Gary, had ever seen his home. Not that there was much to see. A coffeepot and a bed. But it was private.

"You're here. I figure it can't get much worse," she said.

He jerked his head around to meet her eyes and saw the grin pulling at those pretty pink lips. She was teasing him. Teasing *him*. Of all things.

Again, he felt that strange pulse of familiarity. As though they knew things about each other, unsaid and barely recognized.

It made his skin itch. His hands tingled with the sudden urge to reach out and stroke that braid draped over her shoulder. To tug off the band at the end and see what Daphne Larson looked like when she came undone.

His heart chugged hard at the thought, at the image running through his brain of all that hair pouring over her bare white shoulder. Over his bare white shoulders, down his chest, across—

"What's the profit margin on something like that?" he asked, breaking the quiet spell her words had wrapped around him.

"About 110 percent," she said. His jaw dropped briefly and she laughed. "Organic foods are big business, Jonah," she said. "I'm doing nothing but good."

Helen came running back carrying a glass of water, sloshing all over herself as she approached.

"Here you go, Jonah," she said and handed him a glass of water with less than an inch left in it. "And look," she said. "Popsicles. One for each of us."

"How many have you had, Helen?" Daphne asked.

"Mom," Helen said, managing to look arch. "I'm being hospital."

Jonah couldn't stop the laugh and both females looked at him.

That's right, he wanted to say. *The Dirty Developer has a sense of humor.* But for some reason he was pleased to see that surprised, warm look on Daphne's face.

"Well," he said, swallowing the half gulp of water. "Thanks." He handed the glass to Helen and she handed him a Popsicle.

"A green one," she murmured. "The best."

He nearly laughed again, the little huckster.

She was eating a purple one, like the one she'd had before they met on the road and that pretty much indicated which ones she thought were really the best.

"Thank you," he said, bowing slightly. "Green is my

favorite." He turned to Daphne, and tried not to see the golden length of her braid or the wary look in her eye.

He tried, realizing now that it was the smartest thing not to see her at all.

"Thanks for the water," he said, smiling briefly, and walked away from Daphne, her noble and fledgling business and her precocious daughter.

DAPHNE DIDN'T KNOW what to think. Honestly, it was as if her brain had melted in the heat rolling off that man.

She could still smell him—sweat and sunshine and money.

And frankly, that smell really, really worked for her and her overeager, out-of-practice hormones. They were pinging through her bloodstream, heedless of the fact that the man, one, clearly had more issues about his family than he knew what to do with and, two, was not interested in her.

But her hormones called that last fact into question. It had seemed, against all odds, that he'd been watching too closely, the look in his cool, unflappable eyes bordering on admiring—if the Dirty Developer were capable of such a thing.

"Where's he walking?" Helen asked, eating what had to be her third Popsicle today.

"Back to the inn, I guess," Daphne answered, trying not to stare at the man's ass. But cripes. What a tush.

"Wow," Helen said. "That's like a million miles away."

It was. And Daphne knew she should offer him a ride. It was the right thing to do. But…the Dirty Developer? And after talking to Alice this morning, Daphne had learned that not only was he rude to her, but also he'd been keeping Patrick—one of the best men in the world—at total arm's length.

Alice had said Patrick was heartbroken.

Daphne tilted her head as he paused at the bottom of the driveway and opened his Popsicle. He glanced left and gave the iced treat a long lick.

Oh dear God.

"Mom," Helen said, "shouldn't you give him a ride or something?"

"Shouldn't you be doing your homework?" Daphne shot the question back, because her daughter was right and she was stalling a little bit more.

"I was, but then I saw him stop at the For Sale sign." Helen's room had a clear view of Sven's land and Daphne had given her daughter very specific instructions to get her if Helen saw anyone on that land. Daphne still hadn't heard from Sven about her offer and she was hoping to either dissuade other buyers or actually talk to Sven should he happen to visit the land he was utterly neglecting yet not selling to her.

"Why was he looking at the sign?" The man dealt with condos in the city. He'd have no use for farmland in the Hudson River Valley.

"He was stretching," Helen said.

Right, of course, because he'd been running a million miles.

"Finish your homework," she said. "I'm going to give him a ride home." She took off for her truck. "And no more Popsicles."

Moments later, she pulled up next to him while he finished the last of his Popsicle. She leaned across the bench seat to roll down her window.

"Come on," she said. "I'm going into town and I can give you a lift."

He looked at her and sucked the last scrap of green ice from the stick.

Her unruly hormones careened through her system, nearly making her light-headed.

"Thanks," he said, and she popped open the door so he could climb in.

He paused, his leg already inside the cab, the muscle of his thigh tight and defined. Not very hairy, she noticed then wanted to poke out her eyes for noticing. "I'm…ah…kind of gross." He gestured to his shirt.

"Trust me, this truck has seen worse."

He smiled briefly, one of the few he'd flashed. It was as if they were diamonds and he was running out. Which was too bad. His front tooth was crooked, which was startling and heart-tuggingly endearing among all his physical perfection.

He should smile more; it made him look human.

Blushing, she looked away before he caught her staring.

They bounced down the gravel road for a while in the sort of silence that made her regret offering him a ride. It was so heavy she coughed and it sounded like a cannonball.

"Your daughter is something else," he finally said and she leaped on the conversational topic like a rabid dog.

"Yep, she is. She—" oh dear God, how lame could she be? "—really is."

He smiled again, a small gust of a laugh escaping him that did ridiculous things to her heart rate. She could smell the sugary, sweet Popsicle on his breath.

"You and your husband must have your hands full," he said and she whirled because it felt oddly as if he was fishing, as if he'd noted the lack of wedding band on her finger and wondered. But he wasn't even looking at her.

You, she told herself, *are being ridiculous.*

"It's just me," she said. "Me and Helen."

That made him glance her way and his eyes, blue as blue could be, were soft. Warm. Utterly different than she'd ever seen them. Her skin felt as if it might melt and release all this longing she was cursed with.

"You are doing a very good job," he told her. Stupidly his words went right to her soft underbelly and she had to blink back tears.

She was a single mother with a business and a girl who every other day seemed like a changeling rather than her daughter and doubts about her parenting were weeds she couldn't contain with her solo efforts.

"Thanks," she murmured, quickly turning away so he wouldn't see what his words stirred loose in her.

"And you are doing a very good job of being polite to a man you clearly find reprehensible," he said with a laugh. She spun her head only to meet his assessing gaze and crooked smile.

"Not reprehensible," she said and he smirked. "Not totally reprehensible," she amended. "Just…confusing."

It was the truth. What she knew about this man and what had been said about him in the papers didn't seem to add up. This man with a green tongue, and sometimes soft eyes. The man who had made that little bow to Helen and had teased her, who ran miles in the countryside in an old T-shirt, couldn't be poisoning people deliberately. For crying out loud, the guy loved his mother.

Her gut said it wasn't so.

"Doesn't it bother you—" She cut herself off. "Never mind, it really isn't my business." She turned down the road toward the inn.

"Does it bother me what I do? Or does it bother me what

people think of me?" he asked, shifting sideways and taking up way too much space. Way too much air.

"Both," she cried. "If what they say—" Suddenly it dawned on her. He'd all but told her. "It's not true, is it? What they said in the paper."

"Does it matter?"

She could feel his breath, his eyes on her like a warm hand across her skin. Why was he telling her this? Why her?

She stared at him, lost momentarily. Was he, perhaps, feeling this, too? This stupid...yearning.

"Of course it matters." She shook herself free from his gaze. "It's your reputation."

"My reputation is just what people think of me. It's not my job. It's not who I am."

She stopped the truck at her usual space in the parking lot behind the kitchen and shut off the engine. "If this isn't true, you need to clear your name. Tell the Mitchells at least. You need to—"

"Anyone who matters to me knows the truth," he said and got out of the truck. His tanned skin was flushed around his neck and it seemed all too suddenly that he couldn't get out of the truck fast enough.

Bringing up the Mitchells had killed the temporary warmth in him.

He was beautiful, walking in front of her truck with his long legs and fabulous rear end. He was beautiful and, she realized, hugely misunderstood.

She quickly rolled down her window, cursing her lack of power accessories.

"Anyone who matters and me," she yelled as he reached the kitchen door.

He squinted at her and, for some reason, she laughed. It was relief, really, that she wasn't attracted to an utter and total blight on the planet. Instead she was wildly attracted to a complicated, far too handsome man with a freight train of personal issues.

"I know, Jonah Closky," she said. "I know the truth about you."

He stepped toward the door, unresponsive, then turned back to her, smiling. A full smile, as though he was glad that she knew. The blunt lines of his face curved, revealing something unexpected. He had dimples. And laugh lines. And of course, that imperfect tooth that other women might consider a defect, but she considered it delicious.

He was delicious.

Uh-oh.

CHAPTER SIX

SATURDAY MORNING Daphne raced to the Riverview Inn, a woman possessed. She had to convince Tim to go to the School Board Picnic today, and her hopes weren't high that he'd had a change of heart. Helen sat beside her in a state because Daphne had made it clear that Helen would not be spending the night at her father's tonight, no matter how fun it was going to be.

But stupidly, foolishly, more importantly was the front page of the Saturday *Times* that was folded up and practically glowing between them on the bench seat of the truck.

Dirty Developer? It couldn't be further from the truth.

And while she'd been pretty sure she was right yesterday when she dropped Jonah off, she had no idea how misjudged the man was.

How misjudged the man let himself be.

Cripes. She didn't know who was more ridiculous: him for being so mule-headed, or her for caring.

"But, Mom," Helen moaned for the hundredth time. "Dad said that they had the equipment rented for two hours after the picnic ended and that I could play after all the kids had left."

"I know, sweetie, but we have things we need to do at home."

"What kinds of things?"

Nothing.

"Lots. You need to clean your room. And you wanted me to cut out that pattern for the new dress you wanted, remember?"

And your father saw you all last night and I don't need this to get more complicated.

Helen eyed her shrewdly and Daphne focused on the road. "You told me I couldn't have that dress. You said seven-year-old girls needed to have straps on their dresses."

"I'm going to add straps."

"Mom," she moaned.

"Little ones. With bows." Helen loved bows. "And we can make it out of that purple and pink material you loved."

Daphne glanced over expecting to see her daughter in smiles. After going to the drive-in with Jake, Helen had come home with nothing but stories of "Dad did this…" and "Dad did that…"

While Daphne had spent the night working out a marketing plan for her pick-your-own fields and trying not to think of Jonah Closky.

She'd failed. Utterly.

But instead of smiling Helen was solemn. Sad.

"Dad isn't going anywhere, Mom," Helen said and Daphne tried not to sigh. "He's on the Athens Charter School Board and he's running for the county school board next year. How can he go anywhere if he's doing that?"

He left you. Daphne would never say that, but she thought it. *Your father left you when you were so cute, you were smiling and grabbing fingers and lifting your head. He left you when you were barely as long as my arm and your breath was so sweet I couldn't stand to be away from you.*

And he left me. Walked away the second I gave him the chance, saying goodbye when I needed him most.

"I hope he doesn't leave," Daphne said and braked behind the kitchen of the Riverview Inn. "You want to come in?"

Helen was already out the door, no doubt hunting for Josie or Cameron. Daphne grabbed her newspaper and got out. It was still early so she cut through the kitchen, noting that Tim wasn't there. But she'd hunt him down later. She wasn't showing up to this picnic without a date. No way.

The dining room was mostly empty, still too early for many of the inn's guests to make it down for the famous Saturday brunch.

She found Patrick and Gabe and Max lingering over their breakfast coffee. Gabe had Stella in his arms and looked, quite frankly, as though he needed to start mainlining the coffee.

"Hey, Daphne," Patrick said and she had to give him points for trying to be himself. Forcing the twinkle in his eyes, but she could see that the wattage had taken a beating. And she knew Jonah had been wielding the bat.

"Hey, Patrick, guys." She smiled at the Mitchell brothers who smiled back like the big brothers she often thought of them as. "Have you seen the *New York Times* today?"

"Not yet," Max said. "I'm headed in to town in a few minutes. I thought I'd get one then."

"Well, here's a sneak peek," she said and unsnapped the paper to set it on the table between all three of them. And pointed—just in case they couldn't see it—to the headline: Dirty Developer Or Environmental Bastion?

The three men blinked, looked at each other and looked back at the paper.

"Read it to me, Max," Gabe said. "I'm so tired I can barely see straight."

"It says…" She grabbed the paper, her heart pounding. She didn't understand why she was so affected by this news, so on edge by the reality of Jonah. Yesterday she'd suspected the story was untrue, but finding this out was making her crazy. She felt like laughing. Like jumping around screaming, "He's not so bad!"

"Developer Jonah Closky is singlehandedly cleaning up the worst of New Jersey's industrial wasteland," she read. "In the reverse of what was printed about him two weeks ago, the *Times* sat down with the mysterious mogul and found out the truth.

"'It's prime property,' Closky said. 'With views and access to the city. It's just poisoned. We've figured out a way to clean up the soil and make the land usable. Sometimes it takes two or three tries but eventually we get the job done.'

"And Closky has gotten the job done three times with high-rise condos and a fourth being built now after the land has been retested and deemed safe. Moreover, Closky insists on building green—"

"Well." Jonah's voice from the front door cut Daphne off. She lifted her head with a smile, ready to call him out for being so closemouthed. But the expression on his face didn't invite smiles.

Jonah was furious.

All of her jumping glee stopped dead and she couldn't breathe for the look he gave her.

"Someone has been busy," he said, his blue eyes like ice sliding right through her. She felt cold, as if it were February and she was naked. He looked at her as though he hated her.

"Jonah, please—" Iris stood beside him, her hand on his sleeve.

"It's the *Times,*" Daphne said. His eyes were still locked

on hers, although no one else was in the room and she felt as if she'd betrayed him, but she didn't know how. "I was just reading the article."

"Of course." He nodded and finally raked his gaze over his family, lingering on his father, who sat slack-jawed with surprise.

"What you do is amazing," Patrick said. "Why would you let us believe the worst?"

"Because what you think doesn't matter to me," Jonah said.

Daphne sucked in a wounded breath on Patrick's behalf. How much more of this could he take?

"You are a part of this family," Patrick said, coming to his feet, beginning to seem like a dragon about to spew fire and roast something. "You are my son. Whether or not you want to believe that. I want to love you—"

"Dad." Gabe reached out but Patrick shook him off.

"This is me, son. You are not alone." Patrick stepped toward Jonah and for the first time Daphne saw something in Jonah waver. He couldn't quite hold the look of disdain. He couldn't quite keep eye contact with Patrick, willing him away with the chill of his demeanor.

Jonah's gaze dropped to the floor and a muscle pulsed along his jaw. She could see his heartbeat in his neck, pounding for all it was worth.

"We are not out to hurt you more than you've been hurt," Patrick continued, edging closer to Jonah. "I am here. Your brothers. Your mother are all here and you don't have to be so alone."

Jonah's swallow was audible.

"I'm proud of you," Max said and Jonah jerked slightly, as though he'd been hit.

But still he said nothing.

Oh, Jonah, she thought. *Bend before everyone breaks.*

Max glared at Gabe who held on to his mutiny a bit longer before sighing. And finally standing.

"Me, too. I'm—" Gabe swallowed and patted his baby's back. "Grateful and proud of you."

"Me, too," Daphne said, the words flying out of her mouth. Jonah's eyes swung to her and she was scorched by the sudden heat she saw there.

We're more alike than we are different, she realized. That's what the article proved. And that heat in his eyes underlined it. What a change from the chill, the control he had. She wanted to grab him, warm herself as if she'd been cold for years. For too long.

Tears filled Iris's eyes and her fingers, trembling and white, pressed to her lips as if to hold back sobs. Daphne wanted to hug the woman. She wanted to hug all of them.

Particularly Jonah. This felt like the beginning of a breakthrough. A moment that would change everyone's lives.

"I have work to do," Jonah said, removing his mother's hand from his arm. The moment shattered and littered the floor with sharp shards of everyone's expectations.

"But," Iris stammered. "Breakfast."

"Will have to wait."

Jonah kissed his mother's cheek and left the room silent and cold in his wake.

"Wow," Gabe finally said, sitting back in his chair. "That is one stubborn guy."

"Dad?" Max said, watching his father, and Daphne realized the man was crying.

"What can I do?" Patrick whispered, tears running down his face. "What can I do to change this?"

"That's it." Gabe sat, Stella fussing slightly at the movement. "He needs to go. He's not worth all this, Dad."

"Not worth it?" Patrick asked. "How can you say that? He's your brother."

"But he doesn't want to be," Gabe said ruthlessly. "The guy clearly doesn't care."

"That's not true," Daphne said and wished she'd kept her mouth shut when they all turned to her.

"How do you know?" Max asked.

Unerringly Daphne found Iris's gaze. "I'm not sure," she admitted. "I just do." It was in his eyes, in the way he held his head. How hard his heart beat. It was the way he couldn't tell her outright that the article was wrong. And it was in the relief of his smile when she'd guessed the truth.

Iris nodded and Daphne felt a strange buzz down her back, a weakness in her chest that slid down to her stomach.

I know him. I know things about him only his mother knows.

And just like that, she felt the waters go right over her head.

That's it, she told herself. Hormones and stupid intuition be damned. She was nipping this bizarre connection in the bud. Right now. Right here. She needed to get out of this situation. There was no room in her life for this drama. This heartbreak. She had enough of her own.

"I have to go," she said. "Do you know where Tim is?"

"Plotting a vegetable garden with Cameron," Gabe said, pointing toward the kitchen. "On the other side of the hill."

"Okay." She felt as if she needed to run. Needed to put a lot of distance between herself and this place as of ten minutes ago. What had she been thinking running in here like the town crier? And telling him she was proud of him, as if it mattered?

Dumb, Daphne. Dumb. Dumb. Dumb.

She turned tail and left before she made any other dumb moves.

"A LITTLE WARNING, that's all I'm saying," Jonah said to Gary, fighting the urge to kick something. Anything. "I just got ambushed—"

"It's a good article, Jonah. Our phones have been ringing off the hook. Only you would think that something like this constitutes an ambush."

Jonah sighed and stared at the green grass.

The same color as Daphne's eyes.

I'm proud of you.

Lord, he needed his inhaler.

"Still," he said, tipping his head back and breathing deep. "You could have let me know."

"Fine. I'm sorry," Gary conceded, but Jonah didn't feel any better. His stomach twisted and his head seemed three inches off his neck and the pain in his chest... He rubbed it, digging thumb into his sternum but nothing assuaged the ache.

Wow. All of them standing up like that. Saying they were proud. The old man looking as though he could splinter apart with the force of what he'd been feeling.

Jonah stared directly at the sun, searing his eyes. At one time, maybe that would have been important to him. Having their support, watching them stand, shoulder to shoulder on his behalf. When he was ten, making up those stupid stories about a family of lumberjacks, when he'd wished for brothers and a father so hard it gave him head-aches, that's when it would have been important to him. Not now. Having his brothers and father—

He shook his head, wanting to pull the words from his vocabulary. He didn't have brothers, or a father. And what they felt about him didn't change his life at all. Just as he'd told Daphne yesterday, right before he'd almost told her the truth so she'd smile at him.

I'm falling apart, he realized with a sort of panic. Daphne, being at this inn, watching his mother watch him for a change of heart—it was stirring up old demons.

Truthfully what had happened in the dining room had been a dream of his for a lot of years. But he'd grown up and he'd realized that dreams like that—of vindication, of brotherhood, of belonging—weren't productive.

"Yo, Jonah. You there?"

He snapped to in a hurry. Productive. It was time to be productive. "Yeah, sorry, Gary."

"Look, since I've got you on the line—"

"Uh-oh." Something in Gary's voice was ominous.

"We've got two tickets to the New York Realtors Gala next Saturday."

Jonah groaned. "You go, take Carrie."

"I am not the Environmental Bastion. I am the Environmental Bastion's associate. And, Jonah, they want to give you an award."

"What kind of award?" he asked, shocked. He didn't get a lot of those. And considering that most people who would be in that room hated working with him, he could only guess it would be the biggest jerk award.

"I don't know. The letter just says special environmental award. They want some of our good buzz."

"No." He groaned. "I'm serious. Take Carrie, make a night of it. The company will pay for a suite—"

"Carrie's pregnant."

Jonah blinked, stunned.

"You there?" Gary asked.

"Of course," Jonah said, and chuckled. "Congrats, Gary. That's amazing. The world needs more people like you two."

"Thanks, Jonah. That's kind of you to say. But she's been sick, so I don't—"

"Don't worry," he said, feeling the steel bands of his Armani tuxedo close around him. "You really think we need to go?"

"I think if we don't it will be a pretty big snub. We don't need any more real estate agents angry with us."

That was the sad truth, his life depended on those bastards. "Fine." He sighed. "I'll go."

"You can bring a date," Gary said, trying to be helpful. "In fact, it would probably go a long way toward proving to the agents that you are human."

They know I'm human, Jonah thought. *It's been splashed all over the front page of the* New York Times. He'd never felt so naked with all of his clothes on.

And who would he take? Sue had dumped him three months ago, leaving a letter with the usual complaints about his work and communication skills. He hadn't had time to date anyone else and who—

The image of Daphne in red satin, her hair down, sidled into his brain. Daphne wearing high heels, a little tipsy on champagne.

It was a seductive image. It was, actually, a pretty damn hot image.

But it wouldn't happen. He needed to have a conversation with Daphne, let her know that playing around in his life, no matter what her intentions, was not welcome.

She was a menace, that woman.

"A date would keep Tina Schneider off you for the night," Gary said.

"I can handle Tina Schneider." Though that was not a proven truth. Tina was stunning, a former lover and the very new wife of the deputy mayor of New York City—though based on her behavior the last time Jonah saw her, her vows didn't seem to matter to her.

"I've heard they're actually a lot of fun. This one is at the Astoria—"

"It'll be like swimming with sharks, Gary." He heard the clatter of a stone struck by a shoe behind him. He whirled to find Max, steel-eyed and coplike. Like Clint Eastwood in the middle of a dusty road.

"Oh, hey, before you go," Gary kept talking but Jonah barely listened, wondering if Max was going to shoot him or something. "I found out about the land up there. This Sven guy is a little nuts and he's asking for more than it should be worth, but by our standards the land is a steal. I think I'll come out and see it before we make an offer."

"Great," Jonah mumbled. He felt slightly in danger with Max emanating a barely chained, junkyard dog vibe. Jonah had thought all along that Gabe was the threat, but Gabe was a pussycat compared to this guy. Jonah saw that now. Now that he was about to get shot. "Gotta go," he said and flipped his phone shut.

They stood in silence. Spaghetti western music played in Jonah's head.

"What do you need, Max?" Jonah finally asked.

"I need you to give the old man a break," Max said, eyes glittering, mouth hard.

"I'm not doing—"

"You're killing him," Max said, stepping toward Jonah. He did not step away, the air ignited with possibility. A fight would be good. A fight would be perfect! "You don't have to change your name. You don't have to move here. You could leave and never see him again—it would suck— but you could do it."

"What do you want me to do?"

"I want you to acknowledge him. Talk to him. Give him something instead of all this attitude you throw around like you're God—"

"Attitude!" he cried. This time he stepped forward, until only a few inches separated them. "I didn't ask for this. I don't want this. He broke my mother's heart."

"She broke his!" Max retorted. "Don't you get it? This whole thing is rotten. All the way through. For everyone. No one got out safe. Do you think it's easy for Gabe and me to have Iris back here? She *left* us. I was six! Do you know what that means?"

Damn. Jonah had never thought of that. It must have been terrible for them. As hard as what he had to deal with. He stepped away.

"Don't you think we should all cut our losses?" Jonah asked, hoping someone in this family would see sense. Maybe Max could be persuaded to see things his way. "Just let everyone out of this mess?"

Max sighed. "I think it's too late. It's taken us a long time, but something good is happening between Gabe and me and Iris."

"She's not a bad person," Jonah said because he knew how much his mother wanted this.

"Neither is Dad," Max said.

"Then why didn't he divorce her?"

Max paused a moment before slowly saying, "I think he still loves her. I think he thought if he signed those papers, he'd never see her again. At least if they were married, there was some kind of bond."

Jonah wasn't buying it.

"That, and he's a stubborn son of a bitch." Max laughed and clapped him on the shoulder. "Like you."

Jonah wanted to be angry, but Max had insulted him with such affection, he found himself smiling a little instead. "You, too," he said.

I am not going to like the man, Jonah thought.

"We're family, man. Even though you don't want to admit it, you are a Mitchell, too. Which means we're going to have to deal with this mess. All of us."

"Why do you want this so bad? You don't know me. My mom left you when you were a baby. What's in this for you?"

"A family," Max answered as if it were so simple. As if Jonah was the idiot for not getting it. "I spent a lot of time pretending I didn't need one, but you're here and Iris is here and I want you guys."

Jonah looked away, stunned by the honesty.

"Even though you're acting like a whiny baby—"

"Hey!"

"We are proud of you," Max said, punching him in the shoulder, the way Jonah always imagined a big brother would do. "Daphne didn't mean any harm, man. Don't be angry with her," he said, and left.

Jonah stood, immobile, wondering what had happened to his life, how everything had been flipped upside down? And all signs pointed back to a nosy blonde.

"Daphne," he said.

And he went to find her.

"TIM, PLEASE. I'm begging you." Daphne stood in the middle of Tim and Cameron's tomato plants and she wasn't going to budge until she got an answer.

"And I," he said, pushing his glasses up his sweaty nose, "have told you no."

Well, an answer she liked better than that one.

"I cannot show up there alone," she explained for the hundredth time.

Tim reached out, cupping her shoulders, his face sympathetic, but then he gave her a good shake. "Then don't go!" he said. "It's that simple. You don't owe that man—"

"I promised," she said.

"And we always keep our promises," Helen piped up from the herbs where Cameron had taken her to give Tim and Daphne some privacy.

Some privacy.

"Why did you promise?" Tim asked.

To show him I'm okay. That I don't leave. I don't give up when it's hard. That I stick things out.

Those reasons made her seem like a woman who enjoyed taking a hammer to the head repeatedly.

What is wrong with me?

"It's not important," she hedged. "What's important is that I said we'd be there. Today. In—" she checked her watch "—an hour and I cannot show up alone." It would be too humiliating. The reality that she hadn't had a boyfriend or a lover or a single real date since her husband left her was mortifying enough. If she showed up alone, she was sure Jake would know. Everyone would know. Hell, everyone probably did know.

But worse, she worried that if she went alone—if Jake saw her alone—he'd ask for another chance, again. And because she was alone and lonely and because Helen was getting older and life was getting harder, she'd say yes.

She worried she'd be weak. If he kissed her, hugged her, she'd let him back into her life, even for a night. And that weakness would spread, from one minute to the next. To hours and weeks. Perhaps a year.

And he would leave her all over again.

"I don't want to be hurt," she whispered.

But Tim wasn't looking at her. He stared, openmouthed, over her shoulder. Daphne knew only one person who could elicit that kind of response.

"Can I have a word with you, Daphne?" Jonah asked and she closed her eyes on a curse.

CHAPTER SEVEN

DAPHNE LED Jonah away, not wanting to be scolded in front of her child and not wanting to get into a fight in front of Tim and Cameron.

But she couldn't look at him. Not yet. Not until she'd gotten herself under control. She was worked up. About him. About Jake. About everything.

My life used to be quiet, she remembered, stopping on the far side of the lodge, near the forsythia. *And totally under control. My control.* The country of Daphne and Helen had been invaded by an environmental bastion disguised as the handsomest man she'd ever seen.

The man was a menace.

Bracing herself, she met his eyes and saw…nothing. No heat. No icy chill. No lingering effects of the powerful scene in the dining room. Nothing. The man wasn't giving away anything.

"I'm sorry," she said, cutting to the chase. "I shouldn't have pried."

"You spend a lot of time apologizing to me," he said and crossed his arms over his chest. The blue T-shirt pulled against his biceps, his dark hair caught the sun and glittered. For a second he was too pretty to look at.

"What can I say?" she snapped, angry that she still had

these loose cannon feelings for him. She needed them squashed. "You bring out the best in me."

He smiled, not his fully human one, but a small one. A sort of human one. And it only made him cuter. Damn him.

"I have to go," she said, walking away from him. Walking free from his magnetic pull and her hormonal curiosity.

"I heard," he said. "Begging for dates doesn't become you."

She couldn't speak, choking as she was on her ire. On her humiliation. She was a divorced mother who hadn't been touched in years. A small-farm owner with dirt under her nails that she'd never get out. Not without surgery. She was thirty-seven, a size ten and the only dates she could get were ones she begged for. And even those were with gay guys who got hit on more than her.

How kind of Jonah to rub her nose in it.

"You're such a jerk," she finally said, wishing she could think of something better. Something that would pull him apart and hit him where it hurt the way he had done to her.

IT WAS HER EYES. A terrible excuse, he knew. But her eyes made him do it.

The sparkle was gone and all he saw in those green depths was a mild despair. And while she was a menace, he couldn't stand to see her beaten. So he'd made a bad joke about begging for dates. It had been a joke, but she wasn't laughing.

"You're such a jerk," she said again.

And as she utterly eviscerated him with her gaze, he realized he might have overdone it and his joke had become an insult.

"I need to beg for a date, too," he said, quickly, but not

fast enough. She didn't even pause as she walked away from him. Her denim skirt, pleasantly short, flipping up behind her as she went.

"Daphne," he said. "Stop. Please. I'm—" He stopped himself in time. "I have a proposition for you," he said, instead of apologizing. "A good one. Mutually beneficial." Still she kept walking, calling Helen to join her. Ignoring him.

He felt his blood pressure rise, his chest get tight. Offending her had been a stupid idea. Who insults a person to make them feel better? Gary was right, he had the social graces of a water buffalo.

"I'll go to the picnic with you," he said and she only glanced over her shoulder at him. The expression in her eyes like daggers.

"Daphne—" He caught up to her and touched the soft white underside of her elbow. His fingers tingled, his hand went numb and he swore under his breath. This was a bad idea. He shouldn't be setting up dates with a woman he wanted this much. His desire for her, for the soft white skin of her entire body, defied logic. And he preferred his desire logical. Daphne was a tall, leggy blonde, exactly his type. Yet she was so far removed from the women he usually took to functions, she could have been a different species.

"What?" she cried. The look in her eyes was past despair into something wounded and sad and he'd done that. He'd put that pain in her eyes, that doubt in her heart.

"I'm sorry." The words, unprecedented, tumbled out, helter-skelter like animals released from captivity. "I am a jerk. This has been such a weird day and Max punched me and I was trying to make a joke—"

Well, now he was going a bit overboard. He shut up before he started telling her he wanted to talk about his feelings over tea. Maybe watch *Oprah* with her.

"A joke?" she said. Clearly his first apology in nearly fifteen years wasn't enough for her.

"A bad one. But my proposition is good. I will be your date for your event if you go with me to an event next weekend."

Her jaw dropped open. "What kind—"

"Formal. In the city. You'll be away for the night."

"I…ah…I can't just—"

"She'd love to," Tim yelled from behind him, where he apparently was eavesdropping.

"I'll babysit," Cameron yelled.

She put her head in her hands and he literally had to grip his hands together to keep himself from hugging her.

She was so lovely and real. Vulnerable. No woman he'd ever dated, ever seen naked, ever done incredibly intimate things to had ever given so much of herself away.

He liked it. It made him nervous as all hell, did stupid things to his blood flow and heart rhythms, but he liked her this way. Guileless and real.

"Sounds like it's a done deal," Jonah said.

"It's hardly fair," she said, glaring at him. "You're going to a picnic for a few hours, but I am required to go to a formal event in the city—"

"The company is paying," he quickly cut in. "Everything. Clothes, hotel, transportation—"

"Babysitter?" Cameron asked. "I don't come cheap."

"Yes," Jonah yelled over his shoulder. And then he said it again, right to Daphne. "Yes, everything. It was a dumb joke. But you need me right now and I really need you next weekend."

She pulled that lower lip that had been keeping him up nights between her teeth. "Clothes?"

"You can talk to my assistant. She'll get you set up with Armani."

Daphne was positively agog, and he loved it. "Maybe Chanel," he added just to watch her jaw drop.

"What's the catch?" she asked.

Right. The catch. His forte.

"My relationship with the Mitchells is off-limits. You don't ask. You don't read newspaper articles to them. You don't even bother caring what is happening between me and the Mitchells."

"I shouldn't care?" she asked. Clearly the idea was foreign to her, this woman who cared too much about too much.

"Not about me."

He couldn't make it any plainer. Any more clear. Whatever happened between these dates, while he was here at the inn, it would be better—for everyone—if she didn't care about him.

"How do you do that?" She tilted her head, observing him as if he were a strange bug she'd found on her asparagus.

"Do what?"

"Ask me out, offer to buy me expensive clothes yet rope yourself off-limits at the same time?"

I've had a lot of practice.

"Because it's business, not personal. I need an escort to this function. And you need one to this picnic." He shrugged as if it all made sense. And it usually did. He wasn't sure why it sounded so perverse this time around.

"I don't know whether to be offended or sad for you," she murmured.

"Neither," he assured her. "Is it a deal?"

She ran her eyes down his body, slow, as though she were taking off his blue jeans and T-shirt. He had to smile at her audacity, her sheer bravado. But then she looked right at him—through him almost. Past his stupid conditions and catches, his predate speeches right to the ten-year-old boy dying for a father to stand up for him.

"Absolutely," she said and nearly knocked him out with her hundred-watt smile.

PATRICK HEARD footsteps on the steps of the gazebo behind him. He knew it was her, caught the spicy, sweet scent of his wife, felt her calming influence before she said anything.

My wife, he thought, nearly brought low again by the words.

He'd come to the gazebo to clear his head, but he'd come hoping she'd follow.

He scrubbed at his eyes and tried to get himself under control before facing her.

"You don't have to hide your tears from me, Pat," she said. Her cool palm touched his arm, squeezed his hand and he shut his eyes against the pain of everything. A son who didn't want him, a wife who wasn't really his, a situation so out of control he hardly felt like himself.

"Are you okay?"

"You bet," he said, trying to make a joke. "I always cry after breakfast."

"I know this is hard, Patrick. You have to keep at him." She tugged on him so he had to turn. His eyes, he knew, were red.

"I think Gabe might be right," he said, shaking his head, denying her advice, trying not to look at her because she was so pretty. So worried for him and he wanted to touch her so bad his whole body ached. "I think maybe I should let go of this. For everyone's sake."

"No," she whispered and for the first time he noticed her eyes were red, too. Her long black lashes thick and damp with tears.

"You've been crying." His grief broke into a sudden anger. "This has got to stop. We can't keep—"

"You're doing the right thing." She grabbed his arms in a fierce grip.

She's touching me, he thought. His whole body still. *After so long. My wife is touching me.*

"He needs you," she said. "More even, than you need him. What happened today affected him."

"He didn't seem very affected."

"He was. Having a father and brothers stand up for him—" She paused. "When he was a boy…because he was sick all the time, because he was so small he was…picked on. Beat up." She shook her head. "And it got so bad I had to call parents but that made it worse. Finally, when he was ten it stopped. He didn't come home with black eyes anymore but he started to grow this shell."

"To protect himself," he said, seeing it so clearly it was as if he'd been there.

She smiled, but it was bittersweet and he wanted to gather her up, take away the pain. "I don't think he ever stopped growing the shell," she said and started to withdraw her hands and he couldn't have that, so he placed his palm over her knuckles, keeping them connected. Keeping them touching. "He's different with me and with Sheila and his business partner. But the whole rest of the world gets his cold shoulder."

The tears came back and he couldn't handle this anymore. He couldn't be so close and not have her in his arms.

It was stupid. Suicidal. But they were both hurting. What was wrong with comfort? He slid his hands over her cheeks and her breath came out as a sob. Her eyes fluttered shut.

"It's been so long." He barely heard her, could barely hear anything for the pounding of his heart.

She was soft, like silk. Like clouds. Her hair was sleek and it ran through his fingers like water. Her neck was so thin, elegant.

God, she was gorgeous and he couldn't touch her enough to erase the years between them.

She held herself so still, so tense, as if there were electricity running through her body. He wondered, his flesh alive, his heart hammering in his chest, if she felt the same way he did. Like a man waking up after a long sleep.

He touched her. After so many years of dreams, tortured and hot. Unforgiving and passionate. Violent and sweet. He could barely believe it. He ran his thumbs across her cheekbones. Ruffled her wet lashes.

My wife, his heart chugged. Primal ownership forged within the furnace of his body. *My wife. My wife.*

"You did a wonderful job with him," he whispered, not sure of what he was saying, if the promises he made could be kept, but he had to try. "We'll figure it out. We'll make it right."

At this moment, with her so close, he could promise her anything.

"Patrick." She lifted her lashes, revealing black eyes filled with want. A desire he never imagined.

He felt sucker punched.

"You're my wife," he breathed, knowing he was going to kiss her. Unable to stop it. They'd been faithful to each other all these years and he couldn't contain it anymore, years of wanting her pressed down on him.

"You're my husband," she said as if giving them permission to lose their minds this way, to forget what was between them.

He bent his head. And after thirty long years, he kissed his bride. The woman he never stopped loving.

Her lips were still as sweet, her breath still a wine he could drink for days. She fit in his arms, both of them softer than they'd been. But they fit together.

Her mouth opened and he pulled her as close as he could, held her as tight as possible. Carefully he licked her lips and she licked him.

They were careful, all too aware of the years and the desire banked, just on the horizon, but ready to burn out of control.

She moaned and he pulled back, startled, worried maybe he was too rough. Too negligent.

"Are you okay?" he asked, searching her face. *Is this okay?* he wanted to ask. *Will you come to my room?*

Her laughter spilled over them, infused the panic and heat in him with joy and he smiled in response. Kissed her hands. Wanted more, wanted to take off her clothes and lay her down in the sunlight to see if he could remember what she loved. The places on her body—the inside of her elbow, behind her knee—that made her sigh and tremble.

But, perhaps, that was too much for this first kiss. Too much for where they were. For the reality of what was between them. The truth was he didn't know what he wanted beyond this. He wanted to touch her, ease himself in her, but he had no promises. No second chances. Not yet.

"This is crazy," he said. "Maybe too crazy." He was giving her an out—a chance to tell him they were going too fast.

"I miss crazy," she whispered, pushing her hands into his hair and holding on to him with all her might. "I miss you."

"I miss you, too."

That seemed to say it all.

SHOWING UP to the school board picnic with a man like Jonah was a coup comparable to the Girl Scouts taking over Lebanon.

There was no better way to say "I've moved on. I'm not interested," than to show up with Brad Pitt's younger, hotter brother.

Of course, the fact that they were acting like perfect strangers who could barely stand each other did sort of put a dent in that illusion.

But Daphne didn't know how to talk to him right now. They'd covered way too much emotional ground this morning. And sitting in this car with him, having been insulted by him, knowing what she knew and feeling this stupid attraction, was about the most uncomfortable thing on the planet. Like a visit to the dentist and the gynecologist combined in one twenty-minute car trip.

Thank God for Helen.

The little girl talked nonstop about her class—seven students!—and her teacher—a boy!

"Seven students?" Jonah asked. "That's really small."

"Helen goes to a charter school," Daphne explained, watching him sideways to gauge his interest. She didn't trust him, not really, not after that crack he'd made. "We started the school a few years ago for kids who lived in this rural part of the county."

"A rural community school," he said, nodding. "A great idea."

She eyed him skeptically and his lip quirked in a small smile. "My interest is sincere," he said.

"You can be so hard to read," she said, honestly.

"I know," he said. "How about if I try not be so hard to read today and you tell me a little more about this charter school."

Daphne smiled, oddly charmed by him. Stupidly attracted to him. And suddenly, trusting him. The guy was good, she had to give him that.

Daphne launched into an explanation of charter schools and how it was a relief to every parent with a kid at the Athens school, that the school would be absorbed into the County School District starting next September.

"We ran out of grant money and the tuition for the charter next year was going to cost more than what it would have cost all of us to bus our kids to the closest available school," she said.

"Which defeats the purpose of starting a community school anyway," he said, catching on very quick. He faced her, Helen between them on the bench seat, but with his fancy aviator glasses she couldn't see his eyes. Which, maybe, was for the best.

Since she wasn't supposed to care about the man, it would probably be smart if she pretended he didn't have eyes, or a mouth, or pretty hair, or strong hands and veins that—

Clearly that wasn't working.

What am I doing here with him? she wondered. She couldn't even wrap her head around a night in New York with the man—dressed in Armani, no less.

How about that for spontaneous? Her mother was going to fall over in a dead faint when she heard.

And after that speech about not caring about him,

Daphne was stupidly, ridiculously more curious. Because he so clearly needed someone to care about him.

Ah, she was such an idiot. Daphne, Patron Saint of Lost Men.

"So the county absorbs the cost of running the school," Jonah said.

"There will be some changes," Daphne said, snapping back to reality. She turned left at the grocery store and headed up the hill. "But all in all, it's the best thing for our school."

"We have a gerbil in our classroom," Helen said.

"Really?" Jonah asked. "What's his name?"

"Jerry."

"Jerry the Gerbil?" Jonah acted as though he had this kind of conversation every day and once again Daphne was faced with the dichotomy that was Jonah. A man who told her not to care one minute then offered her an all-expense-paid trip to New York in the next breath. A man with a serious lack of social skills—judging by his lame attempt at a joke—but one who took time to talk to a seven-year-old.

Watching him from the corner of her eye, Daphne wondered if he even knew who he was. By denying his family, by living behind this wall that he put between himself and anyone who wasn't his mother, was he aware of all that he could be?

Yes, she thought, forcing her attention back on the road, *all very interesting things that you really should not be thinking about.*

The Athens school parking lot was full and upon seeing the setup in the soccer field Helen nearly passed out.

"Look, Mom. A carousel. And cotton candy," she gasped. "Ohmigod, a jumping castle."

The truck was barely in Park before Helen was climbing over Jonah and out the door, running toward the giant inflatable castle that bouncing kids would no doubt fill with regurgitated cotton candy by the end of the day.

"We'll catch up with you," she yelled after Helen.

"This is quite a setup," Jonah said, taking in the balloons and face painting. "Clowns, even."

She tried to detect sarcasm, or derision, but couldn't find it in him. Which was baffling. She'd braced herself for mockery.

Mockery would kill this interest she harbored.

"Before we go in, there's something you need to know. Helen's father, my ex, Jake is here."

"Am I going to have to fight him?" Jonah asked, scanning the crowd. "Because if I have to fight him, that Armani is getting downgraded."

She laughed, nervous. Then she spotted Jake, three cars away and moving fast, like a democratic ex-wife-seeking missile. "No. But—"

"There she is!" Jake's voice preceded the slide of his arm around her waist. She jerked, stiffened and wasn't quick enough to dodge the kiss he pressed to her hair.

Her blush could have started forest fires.

"Where's Helen?" Jake asked, casual but on point in khaki pants and a red polo shirt. He glanced at her red cotton top and denim skirt and smiled approvingly as if she'd planned to match his attire, as if she was on board with his "united front" campaign.

He was handsome in an all-American way. Brown hair, brown eyes, white teeth. A smile that made him utterly magnetic and nonthreatening. Everything about him seemed dependable, and she'd fallen for it hook, line and sinker.

No doubt in two weeks' time county school board voters would, too.

"She's in the jumping castle, probably," Daphne said, stepping away slightly, far too aware that Jonah was watching all of this, without knowing the story. Without knowing what she needed him for.

"Hello," Jonah said, stepping in. He held out a hand for Jake who had to let go of her waist in order to shake. And as soon as he did, Jonah touched her wrist. A small intimate touch that said so much about other places he might have touched and how often and how recently.

Oh, he knows, she thought, tingling from the touch. *He knows what I need.*

Jake's eyes narrowed.

"I'm Jonah Closky. You must be Jake. I've heard a lot about you." Jonah's smile had an edge, like a slightly jealous new boyfriend, and she wanted to laugh. She actually wanted to giggle behind her hand.

"I am." Jake glanced at her and she smiled. For a moment she wished she could twine her fingers with Jonah's, hold his hand like a new lover. But she couldn't. She wasn't brave enough. Or stupid enough. While it was important that Jake get the message, she didn't need to put on a production.

"I'm afraid you've caught me at a disadvantage," Jake continued. "I thought Daphne would bring Tim."

"Jonah is staying at the Riverview," she said.

"So you haven't been here long?" Jake asked, the real question, "You won't be here long?" imbedded in his voice.

"Not long, no," Jonah said, smiling down at Daphne and she actually averted her face as if embarrassed by all that she saw in his eyes. And she was, because Jonah was making a production all his own. Cripes, the man could act.

"But I do like it here," Jonah said, to her.

"Well." Jake's demeanor had taken a hit and he wasn't beaming quite as bright as he had been. "Enjoy yourself. I'm going to go find my daughter." He shot Daphne a glance, indicating that he would be expecting a better explanation later and left.

Daphne sighed and felt the weight of Jake's expectation and the pressure of the last few months lift right off her shoulders.

"Thank you. That was exactly what I needed to happen."

"Seems like a nice guy," Jonah said after a moment.

"He is."

"So? Why the fake boyfriend routine? What happened?"

Daphne ran a hand over her forehead, shielding her eyes and wished that she had sunglasses that could hide her as well as Jonah's hid him. "He left," she answered.

Jonah glanced at her then at Jake's retreat. "And he wants you back?"

"He's finally gotten into politics. He was deputy manager on George Patzi's campaign for governor. Now he's running for school board and it's only a matter of time before he's climbing the ladder."

Jonah's eyebrows hit his hairline. "He did a good job on that campaign. But what's it got to do with you and Helen?"

"He left when she was a baby." She swallowed, hard, her mouth dry. Spilling the story this way, even though it wasn't her bad behavior at issue, was difficult. She'd put all of this behind her and having Jake back, pretending he hadn't destroyed her years ago, was pulling all her weaknesses and insecurities to the forefront of her life again.

"And he stayed away for the most part. Christmas cards and birthday gifts, a two-week visit in the summer—"

"So, a bad husband and a bad father." The edge to Jonah's voice was real this time, not for anyone's benefit. She guessed that a man with Jonah's father issues would judge Jake harshly.

And, she thought with no little amount of malice, *I'm okay with that.*

But there were so many qualifications to Jonah's assessment. Her mother was right in some respects. Jake might have been a good father if Daphne had given him a chance. But once he left, she made it almost impossible for him to come home.

As for him being a bad husband…maybe she'd been a bad wife. Maybe they'd simply been bad together.

"He says he's here to stay," she said, "that he wants to make a go of it. But I don't know if that's true or if it's because of his reputation and political career."

"Why don't you tell him to get lost?"

Daphne pointed to Helen. She was pulling her father toward the carousel. Her blond hair was lit by the sun, her face barely containing the giant smile. All the love in the world for her dad radiating in her eyes.

Jonah swore.

"Exactly," Daphne said, trying to laugh but feeling strung too tight to make it convincing. "She doesn't think we're getting back together, but she wants us to be friends."

She was unprepared for Jonah's arm around her waist. His heat pressed to her side.

Her eyes fluttered shut in sudden surrender. Not caring about him, she might be able to do. But not wanting him was going to be impossible.

"So, now that I've given your ex something to think about, what do we do at this picnic thing?" Jonah asked, his arm still around her waist, short-circuiting parts of her brain.

Giving herself a slow count of three, she absorbed as much of his warmth as she could, memorized the feel of his arm, the press of his hip and leg against hers.

Then she forced herself to step away. To put as much distance between them as was polite.

He's not for you, she told herself. *He's not staying. You'll only get hurt again.*

"Have fun," she told him, walking toward Helen, who waved at them from the line at the carousel. Jake had been called away and her little girl was dying for someone to ride with.

"Fun?" he asked, not following her.

She opened her mouth to ask him if he knew how, to make light of him, of this whole situation. But when she stole a glance at him, she realized he hadn't been joking.

That buzz ran down her back again.

Jonah Closky didn't know how to have fun.

Cripes, she thought, *does he have to make it so hard to not like him?*

He was being good to her, helping her. The least she could do was teach him how to loosen up.

"Come on," she said, grabbing his hand and tugging him toward the amusements. He resisted, unsure, so she called in reinforcements.

"Helen!"

CHAPTER EIGHT

A HALF HOUR LATER Daphne, screaming with laughter and utterly sick to her stomach, half fell out of the jumping castle.

"Come back!" she heard Helen shout.

"Yeah!" Jonah yelled and someone, she assumed it was Jonah since he was the only adult still left in the castle, tugged on her foot, pulling her back into hell.

"I'm gonna throw up!" she cried and her foot was immediately dropped.

"You okay?" Jonah appeared, red-faced and concerned at her side.

Her stomach did a quick twist that wasn't induced by the bouncing structure.

"I'm good. I just need a second."

"Jonah!" Helen yelled and Jonah smiled.

Flustered, Daphne fiddled with her braid so she wouldn't be compelled to throw herself at the man.

"Gotta go," he said, and ducked back into the castle. There was a roar and the whole inflatable structure shook and shimmied.

Daphne steadied herself and shook her hair out of her eyes.

"What are you doing, Daphne?" It was Jake, holding a

glass of lemonade and giving off the vibe of a disapproving father—not that she was familiar with that particular vibe.

She sighed heavily. She'd known this was coming, but she really didn't want to have this conversation.

"Having a good time," she said, hedging the real question.

"What are you doing with that man?" Jake asked. "Patrick Mitchell's missing son?"

Her eyebrows lifted. "Wow, you've been busy."

"It's all over town, Daphne." He stepped in closer. "And now it's all over town that you two are sleeping together."

"It's not true," she said, slightly pleased that people thought that kind of thing might be happening between a farmer and a guy like Jonah. "He's just a friend."

"He doesn't touch you like a friend. Or look at you like a friend." Jake's jealousy was getting the better of him. It was one of the things that she'd thought was endearing in the beginning of their relationship—proof that he cared about her. But now it was only annoying.

Annoying and insulting.

"It's none of your business," she told him. "You and I are divorced."

"What about Helen?"

"Oh, stop, Jake," she said, rolling her eyes. "Save your devoted husband and father routine for the voters."

His face, earnest and once upon a time beloved, fell. And something like guilt twisted in her stomach. "This isn't a routine, Daph. I'm here. I'm here for good—"

Her snort was unintentional. His earnestness was replaced by anger. He threw the lemonade into a garbage can and leaned toward her. "I know it helps you sleep at night to blame me for everything, and I'm ready to take a lot of blame. But the second things went bad between us you were pushing me out the door so fast my head spun."

"That's not true." She gasped, stunned by the outrageousness of that accusation coming from his lips.

"The hell it is," he said through clenched teeth. "You expected us to fail. You were waiting for me to disappoint you. Just like your dad disappointed you and your mom."

"Oh my God," she howled, struck with laughter and a sudden sharp pain in her stomach. "You should forget about politics and try psychology—"

"Laugh all you want, Daphne, but I'm right. I failed you, I admit it. And I failed Helen. But you never gave me a chance. And you failed me, too."

The jumping castle behind her shook and Helen was belched out, her blond braid unraveling and her face red and sweaty. Seconds later a laughing Jonah jumped out, tripping over Helen.

"Wasn't that fun!" Helen cried, holding on to Jonah as if they were both seasick.

"I have never," Jonah told her, palming the top of her head like it was a basketball, "ever in my life, had as much fun."

Daphne watched the heartbreak cross Jake's face, the pain that seeing his daughter and wife with another man brought to him. None of the victory she thought she'd feel in the face of him realizing that she'd moved on, was there.

She blinked away tears and, as if he knew she needed help, Jonah was there, beside her, his warmth shoring her up. She gave herself a second to believe it, even though she knew it was an act.

JONAH KEPT HIS ARM around Daphne and watched Jake like an eagle. Something had happened. Daphne's laugh was gone and her face was so pale. And Jake had been the cause. Despite joking about it, Jonah could fight Jake if Daphne needed him to.

"Is there a problem?" Jonah asked Jake, whose hands were in fists. Jonah pivoted slightly, leaning toward Jake so Helen couldn't hear him. "Don't do something in front of your daughter you'll regret," he murmured.

Jake retreated, hate and sadness in his eyes. But Jonah had to give the man credit, he pulled himself together and flashed Helen a bright smile. "Having fun, Helen?"

"Yep," Helen said, wary. Jake felt Daphne tense.

Jake gave the girl a big hug. "I love you, hon," he said.

"I love you, too. What's going on?" Helen asked.

"Nothing. I've got to go talk to some people. But after that you and I are going to eat a whole bunch of pizza."

Helen grinned, her world set straight again by the promise of pizza. Jake gave Daphne a long, unreadable look before turning and leaving.

Lord save me from jealous husbands.

Jonah opened his mouth to ask Daphne if they could leave now. The color still had not returned to her cheeks and she was staring at the grass like a woman searching for a place to fall.

She was a tough cookie, but everyone had a breaking point.

And, man, there was something about this woman that seriously pushed every one of his protective buttons. Buttons so small and so hidden he really didn't understand how she'd found them.

"Helen," he said, thinking on his feet, "you need some face paint."

Helen jumped. "I do! I do! Let's go!" She grabbed their hands, pulling them like sled dogs toward the face-painting tent.

Daphne's laughter, bright and real, sent relief and something else, something darker and richer, into his bloodstream. If he had known what was going to happen at this picnic, the emotional quagmire he'd be pulled into, he probably wouldn't have come. But now that he was here basking in Daphne's smile that was as bright as the sun, he was glad.

He could handle this. He could be Daphne's friend and care for her well-being, the way he did with Gary. In fact, this was no different than letting Gary off the hook for that gala next weekend.

He and Daphne were friends. That's all.

But friendship went off the rails an hour later when Daphne introduced him to something called a funnel cake.

"Oh," he said, licking his fingers, while swallowing chocolate-and-sugar-covered fried dough. "This can't be good for you."

"No." She moaned, laughing. "But it's so delicious." She cupped his hand in hers, her fingers warm and soft, and took a bite from the cake he held. The cake they were sharing.

It was unbelievably intimate and erotic, her open mouth and pink tongue so close to his skin. His fingers. He tried to avert his eyes because a button on her blouse had come undone and he could see down her shirt.

You wouldn't look down Gary's shirt, he told himself.

But he looked anyway, and when powdered sugar rained on her chest, sprinkling the top of her breasts, he nearly groaned in sudden agony.

Her lips were dotted with sweet sugar. A spot of chocolate was smeared on her cheek.

I want to lick her, he thought. *I want to cover her in sugar and lick her head to toe.*

The expression on Daphne's face turned hot and he wondered if she could read his mind, or if his desires were just that visible.

The air between them was suddenly too thick to breathe.

"I'm going to kiss you," he murmured as the picnic, the rides, the crowds that had been watching them, all faded away.

"Now?" Her voice cracked and he smiled, charmed so totally by her.

"Too many people," he said, brushing her lips with his thumb then lifting his hand to his lips to suck the transferred sugar.

Daphne's mouth opened and she gave every impression of a woman coming apart at the seams. He liked it. He wanted more of it. Screw friendship, he was going to have her overnight in New York and he planned to *have* her.

"Mom!" Helen screamed and Daphne and Jonah both jumped like they'd been electrocuted.

Jonah's sexy plans went up in smoke as Daphne jerked away from him, putting a good five feet between them, and faced her daughter. "Mom." Helen panted, a smaller dark-haired girl running up beside her. "People are yelling at Dad. You have to come and help him."

"Who is yelling?" Daphne asked.

"Grandpa," the other girl said, staring at the grass as though it might be yanked out from beneath her feet.

"Oh, McKenzie." Daphne sighed, a world of sympathy in that small noise. "Let's go see what's happening."

Helen and McKenzie led them to the food tent where Jake was cornered by a group of six angry people. Jake was holding his hands up, trying to explain something.

As they approached, an older man wearing suspenders yelled, "You can't do that!"

"Now, this has all been explained," Jake said. "Your kids took home a series of notes about the changes to the hot lunch program."

"I haven't gotten any notes!" the old man said, and the crowd rumbled its agreement.

"This is something we should have known about at the beginning of the school year," one woman said, while people nodded. "And breaking the news to us with letters the kids are supposed to bring home practically guarantees we won't get the information."

"Don't you have our addresses? Couldn't you have mailed the letters?" another woman asked.

Something was not going Jake's way. Jonah crossed his arms over his chest and grinned. He'd never thought picnics could be so much fun.

There was something about the guy Jonah really didn't like and having a near kiss interrupted because Jake was getting spanked by a group of angry parents made Jonah like him a little less.

"This was all discussed at the town hall meeting two months ago," Jake said.

"As a possibility the charter school board was looking into to save money before we got absorbed by the county school board," the old man said. "We didn't hear two words about the vote."

"Our meetings are open to the public," Jake said.

"And I work three jobs," a woman said. "Don't blame

your failure to communicate on us. If we had a full-time principal like we used to, this wouldn't happen."

"The full-time administrator position was cut last year in order to save money. Next year, when you are a part of the county, you will have a principal again."

"But not hot lunches," a woman to Jonah's left said. "But you can't cut the hot lunch program just like that—"

"It wasn't just like that," Jake interrupted, laughing in exasperation.

Jonah winced when the woman's face went red. Not a good way to handle an angry crowd, he thought.

"What's going on, Bill?" Daphne asked the old guy.

"Lunch program's been cut at the school," Bill said and Daphne's mouth fell open.

"You didn't know, either?" Bill asked.

"I always pack Helen's lunch," she said. "But she's been asking for double lunches the last week and I didn't—" She stopped, her face turning bright red.

"It's for my granddaughter," Bill said. "Helen's been giving McKenzie her lunch."

"Helen?" Daphne asked, crouching down to face her daughter. "Is that true?"

"She didn't have anything to eat," Helen whispered.

McKenzie gazed at them and Jonah bit back a surprised curse. There was more pain in that little girl's brown eyes than he'd seen—ever. Something terrible had happened to her.

"Don't be mad, Grandpa," she whispered, her eyes lowering to the ground again.

"Baby," he whispered, his voice rough. "I could never be mad at you. But if you'd told me about the lunches, we could have gotten you some food."

"I don't want to be any trouble," she said.

What the hell is going on? Jonah thought.

"Bill—" Daphne laid a hand on his arm.

"Since the accident, I'm working third shift," Bill said, his watery eyes getting wetter. Jonah had to wonder how the guy worked. And where? At his age he should be living on his pension. "She hasn't shown me any notes. She hasn't said a word so I leave her a sandwich. That's it. Because I thought she was getting a good meal at school. Without that lunch—"

Jonah understood the man. Jonah had eaten a lot of sandwiches for dinner when his mom worked nights. There had been a few years when the school lunch program had been the only hot meal he ate. The only vegetables.

He could tell from the looks on some of these parents' faces that the same was true for their kids. This was a rural community where people worked until the sun went down.

He wondered what his mother would have done had his school stopped serving lunch, what further sacrifices she would have made on his behalf.

Jonah removed his sunglasses and looked at Bill, wondering how many more sacrifices this man had in him.

"Jake." Daphne straightened and Jonah didn't recognize this woman, her steely voice, her chin cut from granite, her eyes hard. Her skin was flushed, and she was nearly panting she was so angry, so ready to take this guy apart.

Ah! Business Daphne. Sexy as all hell.

"Daphne," Jake said, relief in his voice. "Please help me explain that for the rest of this year and every year after, there will be no hot lunch program at this school. This is one of the concessions parents are going to have to make to be absorbed into the county board."

"But we're not being absorbed until next year," she said.

"And we ran out of money for hot lunches this year. There's not much we can do." Jake blinked, clearly stunned that Daphne wasn't taking his side. "And the charter school board made an executive decision."

Jonah glanced at the small school and remembered Helen saying her class had only seven students.

"How many kids go to school here?" he asked Bill and Daphne quietly.

"Thirty-five," Bill answered.

"But only twenty eat lunch," Daphne said.

"How much money are you saving by cutting this program?" he asked Jake and all eyes turned to him.

"It's not about the money," Jake said, through clenched teeth. "It's about the board's decision."

It was just the kind of nonsensical, blow-off answer that really pissed Jonah off. These people deserved better than that line of crap.

"What if the parents pay for it?" Jonah asked and the parents around him murmured in agreement.

"Well, it would take a vote and—" Jake hedged, doing a political soft shoe around his answer.

"Months," Bill interjected. "It will take months. Just be honest about it."

"Fine." Jake threw up his hands. "It will take probably two months for there to be a vote. By then school would be out for the summer."

"I'll donate the money," Jonah said. "Two months' worth of lunches for twenty kids."

What could that cost? Fifty bucks a week? Probably less.

There was a stunned silence and finally scattered cheers broke out. Daphne stared at him with her mouth agape. *It's just money,* he wanted to say, slightly embarrassed that he'd made the pledge.

"The cook has been let go," Jake said.

"We can hire another one."

"The kitchen is being dismantled—"

"Ah, don't dismantle it," Jonah said, wondering if Jake had a brain at all.

"This would all require a vote. And as I mentioned before that will take two months." While Jake didn't say it, *asshole* was definitely implied at the end of that sentence.

Jake scanned the crowd, focused on Daphne.

"We don't need false promises from people we don't know. Wealth does not compensate for a community pulling together and creating a personal experience—" Jake continued to talk and Jonah actually felt something in his brain snap.

He was one hundred percent sure he had more personal experience in this area than good old Jake.

"The meals can be made at the Riverview Inn," he said before his brain could catch up with his mouth.

"You don't have that kind of authority." Jake laughed.

"He's right," Daphne said. "You don't. You—"

"I'm a Mitchell, right?" he asked, the words falling fat and awkward from his mouth. "It's what everyone is trying to get me to admit. So, as a Mitchell, I am donating our kitchen—"

The crowd erupted in cheers and Daphne pulled on his arm, yanking him sideways. "What are you doing?" she asked. "Who is going to cook these meals?"

"That Cameron kid." He shrugged. "I don't know. It's macaroni and cheese for twenty kids, how hard can this be?"

"How are you going to deliver the food?" Jake asked, his voice snide now that it was clear he was losing the fight.

"I will donate the use of my truck, Jake." Daphne shook her head at her ex as if he were a misbehaving child she needed to scold. "And I will donate any fresh produce needed."

Jonah smiled at Jake, and slid his arm around Daphne's shoulder, just to rub it in. Despite the satisfaction he had over Jake, a terrible pressure was building in his chest and what he really wanted to do was take back the offer.

Committing to the Mitchells this way was the last thing he needed to do. It went totally against his plan to ignore them until he died.

Back at that inn Patrick was going to celebrate this. This gesture would be seen as Jonah taking a running leap into the bosom of the Mitchell clan.

He opened his mouth, panicked. He could retract some of it. Find another kitchen. Another way.

"Thank you, son," Bill said, grabbing Jonah's hand in his giant paw. Relief and gratitude plain on his face.

Well, crap. There would be no retracting anything.

"You get some numbers to me and I'll take care of the rest," Jonah said to Jake.

Walking arm in arm with Daphne, he shook the hands of the grateful parents as they passed. At his side, he could feel Daphne's astonishment, her gratitude and curiosity like heat from a fire.

"Don't get excited," he told her. "This doesn't change anything. It's a means to an end."

"But your father is going to flip. He's going to assume that—"

"It's Patrick. He's not my father. He's just—" Jonah sighed, resigned to his rash actions. This was so not what he needed to do. "Patrick. And if he'd been here, he probably would have done the same thing."

"Exactly," she said. "Don't you see?"

He stopped and turned her to face him. "I'm serious," he said. "This doesn't mean anything. And you aren't supposed to care."

She stared at him in astonished wonder. Suddenly everything changed, her eyes got sharp and her mouth firm. She clapped her hands on his chest and pushed him backward, behind the school, away from the crowd until his back hit the brick wall of the building.

And then she kissed him.

Kissed him as if he was water and she was dying in the desert. She pressed her strong body against his and pushed the kiss from zero to sixty in no seconds.

"I've got to tell you, Jonah," she murmured, nipping at his lips, with her teeth. The woman could kiss. Her breath was sweet, her mouth hot—he could die like this. "I can manage not caring for you. But you make it really hard not to want to sleep with you."

His eyes flew open. Daphne was laughing but her eyes were very serious.

He slid his hands into her hair, holding her skull in his palms and finally, after waiting what felt like his whole life, he kissed Daphne Larson.

CHAPTER NINE

SHE WAS LIKE LIGHTNING in his arms. And this kiss, this simple series of kisses, got carried away real fast. He found his hand halfway up her shirt and her leg pressed hard against his erection before he knew what hit him.

Brandy—hell, moonshine—had nothing on this woman's potency and he couldn't think. For a second he allowed himself to believe that pulling up her skirt and bending her over some school ground equipment wouldn't be inappropriate. A few more of her breathy gasps and throaty groans and he'd be convinced it had been approved by the school board.

"Hey," he said, pulling away. But she followed, licking his lips, biting his tongue. He groaned and gave in. One more kiss, which slid into about thirty more.

"We have to stop," he said finally, panting hard. His heart thundered against her hand, which was under his shirt. "Seriously, Daph. We're getting out of control here."

Dazed didn't even begin to describe her. She was punch-drunk and he loved it. It turned him on as much as her touch, her kiss, the press of her fine leg against his.

"Right," she whispered, her hands clutching his shirt. "Oh wow." She sighed. He could see her pulse beating in her throat. Her hair was falling down around her shoulders and she didn't seem to know what to do with her hands.

She pressed her fingers to her lips and closed her eyes again; a woman trying to get back control.

As he brushed his hands against her neck and slid his fingers into her hair, she groaned and let her head rest in his palms. Her mouth fell open.

This was a woman on the edge.

And he'd never in his life seen anything hotter.

"You okay?" he whispered.

"No." She tried to smile, but it came out in pieces.

How long had it been since Daphne Larson had been kissed stupid? Or pushed up against a wall and brought to orgasm? Good old Jake didn't seem like the type.

And then, not using his head—which had really been the theme of the day—Jonah decided it wasn't going to be a minute more.

He couldn't leave her this way.

They were at the far end of the school, tucked into a corner between a shed and a recessed entrance. Stepping sideways, he pulled her into the dark doorway, shielded and hidden from anyone who might pass by.

"What are you doing?" she asked.

"Well," he said, leaning against her, aligning his hips to hers and her eyelids got heavy at the touch of his erection. She pressed hard against him and he nearly blacked out. "I think I'll start by kissing you." He tilted her head sideways, brushed back the hair that had fallen from her braid and found a soft, trembling part of her neck, right where it met her shoulder. "Here," he said.

He brushed his lips against her and she melted between him and the door. "Jonah." Her hands drifted under his shirt again, her nails scoring his skin. She stood on her toes and slid open her legs and he fell between them perfectly.

They both gasped.

"And then—" he grazed her knee with his hand, gliding his fingers up her thigh, just under the edge of her skirt "—I'm going to touch you here."

He slid higher, grazing the soft skin of her inner thigh. "And here."

"Yes," she moaned.

His thumb brushed the silk of her underwear. Silk that was damp and hot.

Like a sixteen-year-old kid, he nearly lost it.

"Daphne?" he breathed.

"Whatever, Jonah." She bit her lips and arched back. "Yes. No. Whatever, just…Jonah. Help me."

He forced himself to remember that he didn't have condoms. That they were a hundred yards from a bunch of kids, including her own.

This is, he told himself, *for her.*

And he slid his fingers under the silk, into the fire that was Daphne.

She practically climbed out of her skin, and the choke hold she had on his neck might have killed a lesser man. But he was worthy of the challenge. He braced himself against the wall and rode out the wild beauty that was Daphne coming apart.

Daphne didn't want to open her eyes. Floating on this cloud of sexual euphoria for the rest of her life was a million times better than opening her eyes and dealing with the aftermath of what she'd just done.

It had been years, *years,* since a man had put his hands under her skirt. She'd forgotten how amazing that experience could be. Amazing and electrifying and mind-altering.

Or maybe that was Jonah.

He's leaving, she reminded herself, like dunking her head in a bucket of cold water. *He's told you that. Nothing has changed.*

"Daph?" Jonah whispered, and even the sound of his voice coiled something tight in her.

"Jonah," she croaked and would have cringed if she'd had the ability. It felt as if all her muscles had packed up and left.

She felt his smile against her neck and guessed if he was smiling, reality couldn't be all that bad.

Loosening her grip around his neck, she slowly eased down his body, all too aware of the fact while she had been overdosing on sexual satisfaction, he'd been denied, still hard, pressed right against her hip.

Her eyes popped open. "Jonah—" She reached for him, but he stepped away with a quick smile.

"I'll be okay," he said. He hauled in a deep breath. "In about twenty years." He bent, found her brown sandal and lifted her foot so he could slide it on. His fingers against her ankle, the arch of her foot, was suddenly far too intimate. Preposterous considering where he'd had his hand a minute ago. But having him crouched in front of her, handling her shoe and foot as if she were some modern-day Cinderella made her feel raw.

Uneasy.

She grabbed her other sandal and slid it on. Her brain, apparently asleep for the past ten minutes, woke up and went to work. "I cannot believe we just— That I just—"

"Oh, it was *we,*" Jonah said, laughing. But nothing was very funny to Daphne.

"We could have been caught." She tugged the elastic from what was left of her braid and tried to repair the damage.

"You're right. We could have," he said, watching her hands, apparently amused by the idea. Great, he was an exhibitionist. She should be utterly turned off. She told herself to be turned off. Instead her contrary body flamed a little hotter.

"This was a mistake," she said and that got his attention. The smile left his face. "I don't do this with men I'm not supposed to care about."

She expected that to shut him up. To send him running. He only grinned, revealing that beautiful tooth, the tender reminder of his ordinariness.

"There's a first time for everything." He shrugged, then stepped away from her, turned slightly and adjusted his pants.

She took that moment to bang her head solidly against the plate glass behind her. Stop. Being. Stupid. With. This. Man.

"Don't beat yourself up," he said. "Everyone gets to have a fling with the wrong kind of guy once in a while."

That was the problem. Daphne was pretty sure Jonah wasn't the wrong kind of man.

Yes, he is, she wanted to scream. *For you, he is.*

But why? He was generous and kind underneath his prickly outer shell. They had the same kinds of priorities, the same concerns about the planet.

The guy was seriously skilled with his hands.

"Daphne," he said, touching her braid, the side of her face. Each touch was a brand. A searing pulse against her flesh.

"Try not to think too much," he said. "Give yourself a break. This is fun—just fun—between two people who don't expect anything more than this."

Ah, right. That's why he was the wrong kind of man.

"I don't know if I can do—" she waved her hand in between them "—this." *Just fun,* sex fun, wasn't really her bag. Especially not when she felt such stupid longing and genuine affection for him.

Studying her, his face grew somber. "Okay," he said. "I understand. We can go back to being friends."

"Is that what we are?" she asked, nearly laughing. They insulted each other, used each other and were lying to other people with each other.

"Yeah," he said. "I don't jump around in inflatable castles with just anyone. Come on." He started to walk away. "Let's figure out how to get lunches to these kids before I change my mind about the whole thing."

Friends.

She couldn't quite believe it, but maybe that's what they were.

Too bad she liked him better when he had his hand up her skirt.

IT WAS TWILIGHT when Daphne dropped Jonah off. He circled the vehicle and stood by her open window fighting the urge to kiss her in the bruised shadows cast by the moon over the Catskills.

So lovely, he thought, studying the firm angle of her chin, her mouth that hours ago had been fused to his.

But she wasn't for him. She'd made that clear.

He was still off his stride. He wasn't used to rejection, particularly when it was preceded by a woman practically breaking his neck while she came apart in his arms.

He didn't understand women, he was the first to admit it. He *really* didn't understand Daphne.

He could barely look at her without remembering the feel of that hot, damp silk under his fingertips.

"I'll be by tomorrow," she whispered, trying not to

disturb Helen, who was buckled up and slumped against Daphne, sound asleep. "We can work out a system for delivery to the school."

Daphne smiled, clearly not struggling with being upbeat and friendlike.

Caught between wanting to be just her friend and his own desires to lay her down and have at it like minks, he waved.

That's it. Waved.

Dust trailed behind her truck as she headed to the highway.

He didn't know how to be friends with a woman he wanted so badly.

The sound of people laughing over clanging cutlery drifted from the other side of the inn and he heard the low timbre of Patrick's voice.

Gathering himself to face the music, Jonah walked in the direction of the chatter and found the family on the porch. Even Cameron was there, sitting on the steps looking as though he'd spent the day rolling in dirt.

Delia, whom he hadn't seen but in passing since that first terrible lunch, sat on Max's lap in one of the big rocking chairs. Her fingers absently sifted through the long hair at Max's neck, the touch so intimate Jonah could practically feel it himself, an unwanted tingle across the top of his spine.

Gabe stood, Stella in his arms, beside Alice who sat in a rocking chair, a plate of food on her lap.

Patrick watched over them like some benevolent god. Screws turned in Jonah's stomach.

He heard his mother laugh and located her in the shadows.

Jonah was used to feeling like an outsider, but he'd never been quite this lonely.

Until now.

Watching his mother laugh with her other sons. Her other family.

The blast of pain made him light-headed.

"Jonah!" Iris cried, coming to her feet. Her smile was akin to being wrapped in her arms. She stepped away from them, that other family, toward him and the pain receded. The two of them needed to get out of here. Once he got this lunch thing up and running he was gone and never looking back.

"We were just talking about you," Patrick said.

"I can imagine," Jonah said, unable to keep the sarcasm out of his voice.

"We heard you and Daphne had a date to the school board picnic," Patrick said.

Jonah cut his gaze to Cameron, who shrugged as if repeating what he'd seen had been out of his control.

"We were all trying to imagine you at the dunk tank," Delia said.

"I was imagining you *in* the dunk tank," Gabe said and his wife smacked his arm. "For a good cause," he cried.

"Actually," Max said, his eyes glittering through the twilight, "I'm a little more interested in your weekend trip to the city with Daphne and—"

"It's none of your business," Jonah said, before all of this got more out of hand. He didn't want to talk about her with the Mitchells. She was his secret, warm and arousing, and he wouldn't let these interlopers take that away, too. Not that there was anything to be taken away. And, come to think of it, technically he was the interloper not them.

"Daphne is our friend," Gabe protested.

"Jonah's right," Patrick interjected. "Leave him alone."

Jonah gave the old man a brief nod of thanks because Gabe and Max shut up fast.

"The picnic, actually, got heated," Jonah said and explained about Jake and the angry parents and the defunct lunch program.

"I found Josie's notes from the school tucked into her binder," Delia said. "Otherwise I wouldn't have known, either. Most of the kids throw that stuff away. It's not a good situation because parents rely on that hot lunch."

"Exactly," he said. He crossed his arms, braced his legs, as if he was about to take a punch to the head. They were going to cheer. Applaud. Try to hug him. "Which is why I offered to pay for two months of lunches for twenty students."

The porch was silent.

"To be made here," he finished.

The porch erupted.

"You did *what?*" Gabe cried and it wasn't a happy cry. "Are you out of your mind?"

"You're angry?" Jonah asked.

"Damn right I'm angry." Gabe handed Stella to Alice and stepped off the porch. "I'm working at capacity," he said. "My staff is so overloaded they are ready to kill me. I can't add twenty more meals, five days a week to anyone's job."

"I can hire someone," Jonah said, relieved and stunned that anger was the reaction. He'd expected hugs but maybe he'd get the fight he'd been wanting.

"A stranger in our kitchen?" Alice winced.

"When do you plan on having this work done?" Gabe asked. "My kitchen is fully occupied with the food preparation for paying guests."

"Gabe." Patrick stepped off the porch, too.

"You're going to defend him, Dad?"

"No," Patrick answered and Jonah almost fell over. "He shouldn't have spoken for us." Patrick shot a glance at Jonah and he knew he was being chastised.

A little too late, Dad.

"But it's for a good cause," Patrick said. "Surely there's a way we can make good on this."

"Well, of course there's a way," Gabe snapped. "I just want to hear what Jonah thought he was doing donating our manpower and kitchen without discussing it with us."

"There was no time for discussion," Jonah said. "You all have been trying to get me to accept the fact that I am a Mitchell and I did it."

What am I saying? he wondered. This was what he'd been ready to deny until he was blue.

"And," he continued as if his mouth had no control, "I did what I thought was best."

Gabe rolled his eyes. "Bull—"

"Gabe." Alice broke in. "If we'd been there, we would have done the same thing," she said.

"So would I," Max said. Delia also nodded.

"Me, too," Patrick agreed.

No hugs. No slaps on the back, nothing what Jonah had expected. But the feeling of pride rolled off the porch in a giant tidal wave.

Again, Jonah felt that stupid rush, that nauseating flood of emotion. The night split in two. He was here, wishing this useless, wasted show of unity wouldn't happen, and he was ten years old, wishing desperately that it would.

"Fine. Since you've decided you're a Mitchell when it

suits you." Gabe crossed his arms over his chest. "You gonna cook this food? Because I can't spare Tim."

"I'll do it," Cameron piped up.

"When?" Gabe asked. "You aren't dropping out of school."

"I'll come before school." Cameron stood. "It's gonna cost you."

Jonah nearly laughed. "I can imagine."

"Cameron," Alice said. "You'll need to figure out recipes and budgets. It's for kids so it's going to take some work. Are you sure you want to take all that on, on top of school work?"

"When I was in grade school, after Mom left, hot lunch was the only meal I ate," he said, looking at Jonah as if he identified the same truth in him. "Kids need lunch."

Jonah nodded, touched by the kid's help. "Kids need lunch," he echoed.

"Okay. Where is the food coming from?" Gabe asked.

"Daphne is donating some and I am paying for the rest."

"How is the food going to get to the school?"

"Daphne donated her truck."

"You'll drive it?"

"Someone will."

"No one here has the time. You can't go speaking for us," Gabe said. "Committing us to—"

"Relax, Gabe," Patrick said and Jonah refused to see the pride in him. The respect. The gratitude. "It's done."

Gabe sighed heavily and stomped up the stairs. "Fine," Gabe said. "I'm prepared to pick up the pieces when this guy leaves us high and dry." Gabe shot Jonah a damning glare. "He will," Gabe said to his father. "You've got to come to grips with this, Dad. He will leave."

At least we agree on that, Jonah thought, finding it strange that Gabe was the only one who saw things his way.

"He's not leaving now, son," Patrick said, smiling sadly. "So let's go easy on him until he does."

Gabe shook his head in disbelief. Alice stood, the baby on her shoulder, to kiss his cheek. To smile at him with love in her eyes.

Again, Jonah felt as if there was a wall of glass he pressed against. Watching, always watching.

"Come on," Alice said to Cameron. "Let's get started on those recipes. The sooner those kids get lunch, the better."

The rest of the family followed into the inn as well, until it was only Max, Mom and Jonah left.

And Max was in his Clint Eastwood mode.

"Daphne is our friend," he said, and Jonah had to give the guy points for cutting to the chase.

"She's my friend, too," he said and Max laughed. The laughter almost had Jonah telling the truth—they were friends despite his best efforts to make them something more.

Still, this little warning of Max's was the height of ludicrousness considering Daphne had no intention of letting Jonah near her body, much less her heart.

"Sure she is. But I'm telling you, if you hurt her, I don't care that you are my brother."

The threat of bodily harm didn't need to be spoken aloud.

"And I'm telling you," Jonah said, not backing down, even though Mom was there. The word *brother* sent something sharp through his nervous system, electrical spikes that made him see stars. "It's none of your business."

"Max," Delia called from inside. "Josie needs help with her math homework."

"Be right there," Max said. "It's cool what you did," he

said to Jonah. "Speaking up for us like that. Gabe's just mad because he wasn't there to be the hero."

Then Max was gone before Jonah could insist that he was no hero.

"Well, well," Mom said, her eyes twinkling as she crossed the grass. "This is quite a development."

"Nothing's changed, Mom. I did what I had to do."

"So acknowledging your connection to the Mitchells was just a means to an end?"

"Yes," he said. "That's it exactly. But what are you doing, Mom?"

She tilted her head. "What do you mean?"

"Sitting here, pretending like you belong here?"

Pain flickered in her eyes and he was sorry about that, but things were getting out of control.

"Are you saying I don't?"

"The guy didn't want you, Mom."

"Maybe he does now. Maybe they all do."

"Are you forgetting that you have a life in Arizona?"

"What life?" She laughed and Jonah felt a serious panic gripping him. She sounded as if she was already putting distance between herself and the real world.

"Your friends, your pottery, your—"

"Loneliness? My empty nights? My empty bed?"

"Mom!" he cried. "You cannot mean to have a relationship with this man—"

"I already do." She laughed slightly as if the situation were all so absurd to her. He had to fight his instincts to pack her into his Jeep and drive away, leaving this place and these people in the dust, before his mother lost any more of her mind. "This man is my husband."

"Right, because the bastard couldn't be bothered to

divorce you. That's how little he thinks of you, Mom. That's what we mean to him. We're afterthoughts, Mom. We're nothing to him."

She held up her hand and it shamed Jonah to see it tremble. He'd never spoken to his mother this way.

"Stop," she said in a burning whisper. "Before you say something you'll regret."

"I don't want you to be hurt."

"I'm already hurt." Her voice sounded rough and foreign.

He closed his eyes on a curse. He didn't mean to do this, insult two wonderful women in one day.

What is wrong with me?

"There is no reward without risk, you know that," she said, touching his cheek. "It's the same thing in love."

He shook his head. It was a bad ratio in love—too much risk and, from what he'd seen, not enough reward.

But he'd said enough for one night, so he pulled his mother close and apologized. For the second time in fifteen years—both in one day.

Somewhere, pigs were getting ready for takeoff.

CHAPTER TEN

SUNDAY MORNING, with Helen at her heels, Daphne opened the door to the Riverview Inn kitchen, and found it full of women: Delia, Alice with Stella, Iris, Josie.

The lone spot of testosterone, Cameron, sat at the butcher's block like some kind of time traveler in the wrong era.

"Those are ten good menus," Alice said. "You need to talk to Jonah about the budget and talk to your suppliers—" Cameron was gone, notebook in hand, before she even finished her sentence.

The women all laughed in his wake.

"What's so funny?" Helen asked her friend Josie, too young to understand how Cameron must have felt surrounded and outnumbered.

"I don't really know," Josie admitted. "But I made sure that Cameron had noodles with cheesy peas on the school menu. And no spinach." She looked at her mom from the corner of her eyes and Daphne bit back a smile.

The girls high-fived and ran out of the kitchen, talking about what else was going to be served at school, hopefully come Monday.

"You guys have been busy," Daphne said, watching the swinging door shut behind her daughter. None of the remaining women responded and when she glanced around to see if she'd been deserted, she saw Iris, Delia and Alice sharing looks over the tops of their coffee cups.

"What?" Daphne demanded, hating to be the butt of any joke.

"You've been busy, too," Alice said in such a knowing way that Daphne burned with a sudden blush.

Had Jonah told them? she wondered, appalled and embarrassed. "Wh-what do you mean?"

"New York City?" Alice asked, putting down her cup.

"Armani?" Delia asked, with equal parts astonishment and envy. "How did you do it?"

"That is a very good question," Iris said. "How did you get my son to go to a school picnic? Not to mention volunteering on behalf of a family he hates, to coordinate lunch efforts for a school?"

"Well." Delia laughed, hoisting herself up onto the counter, "I was really more interested in how you got a man to pay for an Armani evening dress, but—" she waved her hand "—you can answer those first."

Relief blew through Daphne. "It's business, that's all. He helped me and I am helping him."

"That explains the dress," Iris said, arching an elegant black brow, "but not his behavior."

Daphne sighed and decided to tell the honest to God truth that had kept her up too late at night, that had dogged her this morning walking the apple orchards.

Her body, her blood, her lust had all been jump-started, and she couldn't stop the constant hum in her nerve endings.

About the only thing that had been acting as an effective cold shower was wondering *why* he'd done it? Why he'd pulled her into that dark doorway? Why he'd put his hand up her skirt? Why he'd torn the carefully protected and iron-clad fibers of her world into pieces?

"I have no idea why Jonah does the things he does," she said.

Iris laughed. "Welcome to life with my son."

Daphne jerked at the implied intimacy of her words. Thoughts of Jonah were needles under her skin, constantly poking and abrading. And she worried that life with him was something she, like an idiot, wanted.

Stella fussed, lifting her fuzzy black head from her mother's shoulder. Upon seeing Iris, the baby smiled and it was as if Iris broke open and sunlight shimmered from within her.

"Come here, baby girl," she said and Alice handed Stella over with a grateful smile.

"She's been eating around the clock," Alice said. "And Gabe is in a conference call with a bride and groom for next year."

"Well," Iris cooed at Stella, "let's just give you a break. I'll take her for a while." Iris waved halfheartedly at all of them as she left the kitchen. Her eyes were for Stella and Stella alone.

"Iris is so good with her," Daphne said.

"Yeah, yeah." Alice jumped up on the counter next to Delia. "We can talk about that later. Let's talk about you—"

"Me?" Daphne asked, stalling for time.

"Yes," Delia agreed, her Texas accent more pronounced than usual. "Let's talk about you and the Environmental Bastion."

"There's really nothing to say," Daphne said and wondered how long she could keep this act up. She wasn't good with secrets. Or lies. Or pretending that yesterday her world hadn't been utterly rocked. For the first time in long, long years.

"*Riiight.*" Alice jostled Delia. "You've got a funny look in your eye, Daphne Larson, and something tells me it's not vegetables that put it there."

"We're friends," Daphne protested, her voice sticking slightly on the word. "That's all."

"The guy is hot," Delia said. "And from the way he told Max off last night, he's feeling something more than friendship toward you."

"What did he say?" Daphne asked far too fast, and far too eager. Alice and Delia, the she-devils that they were, laughed. The jig was up.

"I knew it!" Alice crowed. "What happened? Tell us. We need details."

Daphne groaned. "Nothing." She smiled, watching them from the corner of her eye. "Much."

They leaped off the counter at her, but Daphne held firm. She would have died if Jonah had told anyone and she could imagine the überprivate Jonah would feel the same way. "The important thing is that it's not going to happen again."

"Why not?" Delia asked.

"Because there's no point. He's leaving." It made perfect sense to her, but they stared at her as if she'd just said he was a donkey.

"It's not marriage," Delia said, and she had some serious issues about marriage. "It's a night. I mean, I'm not telling you to go out and sleep with the guy if you don't want to." She paused. "Do you want to?"

Daphne couldn't quite put her urges into words so she just nodded. "But what's the point, if nothing comes of it?"

"Oh, sweetie." Delia pulled on Daphne's fat braid. "You don't get out much, do you?"

Daphne stuck her tongue out at Delia.

"It's just fun," Delia said. "A man like Jonah. A night in the city—"

"You are going to New York with a man you want to sleep with," Alice interrupted, taking charge in her practical list-making way. "Overnight, in a fancy hotel in a spectacular dress and you're going to wave good-night and sleep alone?" Alice demanded. "Are you nuts?"

"No. I'm—" Careful. Scared. "—nervous," she finally admitted. "I've slept with two people in my life and one of them was my husband. I'm so out of touch, I'm afraid that I'll get caught up in everything, the romance of it all. And I'll forget that it's not for real. And I'll get hurt somehow."

"But you said it yourself—" Alice rubbed her shoulder "—the man is leaving. There's no way you can forget that."

That stroke of insight exploded in Daphne's brain, reorganizing things. Reducing these mountains to molehills.

"You're like Cinderella, honey." Delia stroked her hair. "A night so far removed from your regular life, why wouldn't you just go with it?"

Right. Why not?

Reasons pounded in Daphne's brain—but they seemed silly, sort of, now.

It was a night at a ball, in a fancy dress, with a sort of prince.

"He's leaving," she said, as if just discovering it herself.

"That's right," Delia said. "Probably, never to be seen again the way things are going around here."

"It wouldn't kill me to have some fun?" Daphne didn't mean it to come out like a question, but it did.

"No," Alice said, "it wouldn't. In fact, I think it would

do you some good. Drink champagne, be gorgeous, have sex with a handsome man. Remember what it's like to be a little out of control."

Daphne sucked in a deep breath. Out of control did not sound fun. Champagne did, though. And so did the sex.

I can do this. I can do this and still be in control. Laughter burst out of her like a geyser. "I can do this!" she cried.

"Atta girl!" Delia agreed. "Now, what's the dress like?"

"I don't know. I'm supposed to talk to his assistant tomorrow."

"Ask for something red," Delia told her.

"And strapless. You have arms and shoulders most women would kill for," Alice said and Delia nodded in hearty agreement.

"You'll need a facial," Delia said, her own alabaster skin practically glowing. "We can reduce some of the chapped skin on your cheeks. And even out the sunburn." Delia grabbed her hands and clucked sadly over the calluses and blunt nails. "Ask his assistant for gloves. High ones. Black."

"*Ooohhh,*" Alice cooed. "That'll be sexy."

Daphne felt sexy just thinking about it.

"Now—" Delia got very serious "—sweetheart, times have changed since you were married."

"Tell me about it." Daphne laughed, though she was slightly nervous about the look in Delia's eye.

"Have you ever gotten a wax?"

Daphne looked to Alice for clues. "A waxed what?" she finally asked.

Delia's eyes twinkled with devilish delight as she tugged Daphne toward the spa. "Come with me. It won't hurt a bit."

Daphne shot a panicked look at Alice in time to see her wince.

IT WAS REMARKABLY EASY. In fact, putting together lunches for twenty kids was exactly as easy as Jonah had thought it would be when he opened his mouth at the picnic on Saturday.

Two days later he had a budget, dairy, meat, fruits and vegetables coming in at a discount. He'd even woken up early on Monday morning in case Cameron didn't show up and he had to open a couple of boxes of macaroni and cheese.

But the kid was there. And since he was up and the coffee was on, Jonah cut up fruit to go alongside Cameron's pasta with ricotta cheese, lemon, ground turkey and peas.

Daphne roared into the parking lot with her truck at about eight o'clock but she left soon after, getting a ride back to her farm from Max.

"I'm sorry," she said to Jonah. He was mesmerized by the dirt across her nose. "I wanted to go with you, but we're having some problems with the irrigation in the greenhouse."

"Can't have that," he said, washing his hands free of grape juice, terribly aware that he smelled like fruit. He was even more terribly aware that she smelled like grass. Warm, sweet grass.

And that smudge across her nose… He wanted to take her to his cottage, climb into a hot shower with her and scrub her down. All over.

Overkill for a smudge, but what was a guy to do?

"It's fine," he told her when she hesitated. "I can deliver the food on my own."

"Okay." She smiled and for a moment she seemed balanced precariously on some decision, hesitant and careful. He thought, maybe, she was going to kiss him.

God, yes, please. Kiss me.

In the end she only squeezed his shoulder, her hand strong, her finger brushing the flesh of his arm under the sleeve of his T-shirt.

Better than a good-buddy punch, but not quite like the dreams he'd been having about the woman since Saturday.

Not at all like those.

So, he and Cameron loaded up the truck with the pans of food. Two small pans, dwarfed in the truck bed. He could have carried them in his lap. It seemed ridiculous, all these problems for so little. Forty cups of food. One cup of pasta and one cup of fruit for each kid.

Then Cameron checked his watch, swore and ran over to the crappy hatchback he babied as though it were alive— or at least made in the past ten years.

"I'm late for school!" he cried. "Alice will kill me if I'm late again."

Then he, too, was gone.

It was just Jonah, the truck and the food.

He knew where the school was. He just didn't know where it was from here.

"Problem?" It was Gabe, standing in the kitchen doorway, holding a cup of coffee and wearing a smirk. Sunlight hit the guy's hair and practically gave him a halo.

Crap. Gabe was the last guy he wanted to ask for help, but there was no one else available. He chewed on his tongue, swallowing everything he wanted to say, concentrating on the sacrifices everyone had made to get them to this point and—

"You are one proud SOB," Gabe said, draining his cup and setting it in the kitchen. "Come on, I'll show you where the school is."

He held up his hand and Jonah tossed him the keys over the truck bed.

Yep, it had all been easy up to this point.

"Did Cameron get to school on time?" Gabe asked after they'd pulled away from the inn. Jonah noticed a big splotch of baby spit-up on Gabe's black shirt, ruining his hard-ass act.

"Yeah," Jonah answered. "He said Alice would kill him if he was late again."

Gabe smiled but didn't elaborate.

"What's the story with the kid?" Jonah asked.

Gabe glanced at him then back at the road. "What do you mean?"

"I understand he's employed here, but between here and school when does he ever go home?"

"This is home," Gabe said. "Not officially, but he's got a place in the lodge whenever he needs it. He worries about his dad so he goes home most nights to make sure the guy hasn't finally drunk himself to death."

Jonah sucked in a quick breath and gazed out the window, the pieces coming together. Hot lunches. Mom gone. The ludicrous hourly wage he'd wrangled out of Jonah. The kid was practically on his own. Except for the Mitchells.

I will not like these men, Jonah told himself.

Gabe's laughter turned his head.

"What's so funny?"

"I was telling Alice last night that you would be so much easier to deal with if you weren't turning out to be a nice guy."

Jonah's skin chafed at the thought of being *a nice guy* while his neck flushed at the rusty praise.

"Max says you agree with me," Gabe said when Jonah didn't respond to him. "You know, about how we should go our separate ways and stop trying to force ourselves to be a family."

"I do agree with you," Jonah said, wondering what happened to his fervor for that plan. Mom wanted to be this guy's mom. And Max's. And Stella's grandma. Jonah was beginning to feel like an ass trying to deny her that happiness.

Gabe nodded and turned past the grocery store where Jonah had picked up citrus fruit and pasta for the lunch. The school came into view.

Straight into town and left at the grocery store. I think I can handle that.

Gabe parked near the scene of Daphne and Jonah's make-out party, but didn't move. He simply stared out the windshield as if facing a heavy decision.

"I think I've changed my mind," Gabe said. The hair on the back of Jonah's neck lifted. "I think our folks want this. My wife wants this. So does my...our brother."

Gabe rubbed his hands over his face and through his hair, a gesture Jonah recognized as one of his own.

"What do you think?" Gabe asked him. Really asked him, as if whatever Jonah might say Gabe would listen to. Consider. Allow to affect him.

And suddenly, that gesture from the big brother he didn't want moved him more than the shows of support Patrick orchestrated.

A lump filled his throat and the inside of the truck was too hot to tolerate. Cold sweat ran down his sides. "I'll be right back," he said and left the truck before he did something stupid.

"WE HAVE TO STOP meeting this way," Patrick said, pressing a kiss to his wife's bare shoulder.

"Then you will have to stop sneaking into my cabin." She laughed, flinging her arms out on the bed.

A week of lovemaking, of sneaking into her cabin at

night, of finding her alone in the gazebo in the afternoon. A week of relearning this woman's body and sex. He felt like an addict. He couldn't stand to be away from her and, those few moments he was, he spent planning what he'd do to her once he got his hands on her again.

Thirty years of celibacy had given him a filthy mind and his wife was little better.

Even now, tired from feeding this addiction as though he were a man half his age, he wanted her again.

Couldn't do much about it, but he wanted her. And it filled him with a powerful, virile glee, to want again. He longed to throw her over his shoulder and take her to a cave somewhere with a bottle of Viagra and food for a month.

Moonlight lay over her like a silver veil, turning her body's now familiar terrain into mysterious, uncharted topography. Her neck beguiled him, her sharp collarbone pressing against the thin white skin tempted him. Her shoulders, strong and wide, rising from the sheets like Venus from the waves, humbled him.

He leaned over her, pressing kisses along those parts of her he most admired. Tugging down the sheets, he searched for new territory to adore.

"Patrick?"

"Hmm?" He'd reached the top of her breasts, full and round and womanly in a way that made him ache. And her nipples—

"Patrick." She pulled the sheet back up and ducked her head to look at him.

Uh-oh. He knew that look. Hadn't seen it in years, but he'd recognize it anywhere. His erection, tentative and tired, relaxed gratefully against his leg.

"What's wrong?"

She wants to end it. He could feel it in his gut and, while he hadn't thought far enough ahead to foresee this, he wasn't surprised. He was suddenly sick to his stomach, but he wasn't surprised.

She was going to leave again, and it felt like his heart had hardened to stone in his chest.

"Have you told the boys?" she asked. "About us?"

"No," he said carefully. Nor was he ready to. This was his secret, his and Iris's. Telling the boys would require them to explain the things he was choosing not to think about. Such as, what was he thinking? Where did he think this was going? Was he planning on asking her to move here? To share a married life?

Thinking about those things would require him to ask her and he wasn't ready for her answers. Not if they weren't what he wanted to hear.

And, truthfully, outside of those soft cries she made from the back of her throat when they had sex, he wasn't sure what he wanted to hear.

She nodded. "I think that's for the best, don't you? For right now?"

"Why are you thinking about this?"

"Jonah." She shook her head. "I think if he knew about us—"

"He would be mad?" Patrick laughed. "It would be hard to tell the difference."

"He would be hurt. He would see this as a choice." Her black eyes were liquid, gorgeous and honest. She pressed her hand against his chest, caressing the skin over his heart, her thumb grazing his nipple. "You over him."

Oh man, was there no way to turn in this situation without someone getting hurt?

"Well, we won't tell anyone," he said, pulling the sheet down her body, until her breasts were revealed. Heavy and full. So beautiful.

"It will be our dirty secret." She smiled at him as his erection, rested, got back in the game.

THE MOONLIGHT limned Daphne's asparagus, turning them silver in the magic hour just past twilight. She walked the narrow rows, out of habit, without thinking. The crop was mostly gone, the land ready to be tilled, ready for rest.

Her strawberries were coming in, she could see them like hidden rubies one field over. If she had more acreage she could make the farm more of an attraction. Parents and kids could spend the day harvesting fruits and vegetables. She could have a jungle gym and sell cider in the fall. She could expand the orchard, the berry fields, maybe even the greenhouse.

But even without the land, she had to admit business, she thought with a happy sigh, was booming. In a few months she'd have the fall crop then move to the greenhouse and the blackberries that sold like diamonds in the winter.

Strange that success felt so lonely.

Helen was gone—pizza and bowling with her father in Athens. Jake had backed off since the picnic, making their relationship far more comfortable for Daphne.

But, as she had been since he'd come back, Daphne was alone on a Friday night.

Jonah. Her body sighed his name. Her house was empty. The night was ripe and lush. She was practically hairless, thanks to the sadistic Delia.

But bringing him to her home, making love to him in

her bed, that would be a mistake. That would bring him too close to her world.

New York. Cinderella. A night away from her life. That was what she could handle. Anything else would court disaster.

Even thinking of him, here among the last of her asparagus, seemed like an invitation she shouldn't be offering. But now that she'd made this decision about tomorrow night, about sex, thoughts of Jonah were guests that wouldn't leave. They followed her around the kitchen, through the fields and greenhouse. They rode beside her in the truck when she took Helen to school, they slept beside her in her bed, breathing fire and taking up too much room.

Tomorrow night, she thought. Her entire body hummed at the thought.

She wasn't able to even daydream about her night in New York City. She couldn't imagine the dress, or what she'd look like or the hotel. She couldn't figure out how she was going to kiss him, touch him. How she would get him into her room.

That's how foreign this experience was. It was a blank page. Her body already felt like someone else's. Her face was so smooth, so clear—the chapped sunburn erased under Delia's creams. Even her hands were better, though the gloves would still be a necessity.

As for the wax…well. Wouldn't Jonah be surprised.

Her body burned hotter at the thought. The secret naughty thrill of knowing what her sensible cotton underwear covered.

"Stop it," she muttered, tired of running over this in her head. Turning left at the end of the field, she came to the fence that separated her land from Sven's.

She eyed Sven's property and wondered what more she could do. She'd called him four times today, alone. Not that it seemed to do any good. At this point, the old man could probably arrest her for harassment.

Grasshoppers buzzed against her leg, filling the night with familiar noise.

The buzzing in the pocket of her coat and sudden ringing of her cell phone added to the night music.

"Hello?" she answered, expecting her new delivery guy.

"Daphne Larson?" a male voice, heavily accented, asked, and she realized it was the elusive Sven. Apparently that fourth call had done the trick.

"Sven! I'm so glad you—"

"I have had another offer for the land. I am taking it, so stop calling."

"What do you mean you've had another offer?" Daphne tried not to yell at Sven, but really this was too much. Her hand hurt she clenched the phone so hard.

"I have had another offer," Sven repeated, a regular font of enlightened information. "Someone called two days ago and I told them I was selling the land. The man assured me that he could match what you offered and asked me to name a price. I thought it was a joke."

"How much did you tell him?"

"A million dollars."

Daphne stumbled. Surely, someone hadn't paid that exorbitant amount.

"We settled on a half million," Sven continued.

She wasn't sure if perhaps the buzzing in her ears, or her teeth cracking from biting down on them too hard, or even Sven's thick accent made her hear that amount wrong. Because there was no way someone was going to pay half a million dollars for twenty acres and three falling down buildings close to the middle of nowhere. The land had limited value to anyone but her.

"I'm sorry," she said. "I think I misheard you."

"You did not," Sven said. "Half a million. Can you match it?"

Of course she couldn't. But she thought of her jungle gym and hot cider.

"Not right now, but perhaps in—"

"I am sorry, Ms. Larson. I like you. I do. But I am a fool not to take this offer."

The line went dead. Her apples. The you-pick business.

Was it always going to be like this? Second place? Never enough.

Who would pay that much for land out here? Maybe Sven was making it up, fishing to see if she would more than double her offer.

That had to be it. The land was barely worth what she had offered.

Slimy bastard, she thought, staring down at her plants. Her soil. Was faking an offer even legal? She doubted it.

Jonah would know the answer. She gripped the phone in her hand. She could call him, ask him to come over to discuss real estate…and somehow manage to get him to put his hand under her skirt again.

She couldn't even muster a smile at the thought.

Her heart was heavy and disappointment sat hard on her. She'd wanted that land, had started to think of it as hers.

"Cripes," she muttered and walked through her strawberry patch toward the house. Pushing away thoughts of Jonah, of Sven's twenty acres, of a future that wasn't, in the end, supposed to be hers.

CHAPTER ELEVEN

THE COUNTRYSIDE flew by in a green ribbon outside the passenger window of Jonah's Jeep and Daphne watched it as though, at any moment, it might change, as though New York City would explode outside the car.

"Are you all right?" Jonah asked. They'd been driving for half an hour and, so far, conversation had been about as lively as a funeral.

How are you?

Good.

Good.

School lunches are going over well.

Too well. More kids have signed up.

Good.

Good.

Cripes, I'm so wound up, she thought, her mind working far too much. She wanted to run for miles. Take a cold shower. Anything to work off this steam that built in her.

She unrolled the window.

"I'm good," she said with a quick smile, then cringed at their mutually limited vocabulary.

"Is it Helen?" he asked. "I mean, does it bother you to leave her alone for the night?"

She shook her head. "Cameron's there until dinner, then

my mom is going to spend the night. Trust me. Helen is thrilled. I'm just a little preoccupied with work."

"Tomatoes giving you trouble?" he asked, but his smile was so sincere she knew he wasn't making fun of her.

"Strawberries," she joked. "They are trying to unionize."

"I've always said you could never trust a berry."

"Actually…" She took a deep breath, wondering what she was doing. This whole New York experience was supposed to be a moment out of the ordinary. Yet, here she was pulling real life into this car with them. "I had a bit of a setback. I was trying to buy some land next to mine and I found out last night it sold."

"Sold?" he asked, his eyes sharp, his voice sharper, and she was glad for his reaction on her behalf. Her mother had simply said, "You win some, you lose some," but this fierceness from Jonah was very nice.

"Yeah, that farm beside mine. Someone paid a small fortune for it."

"Do you know who?"

She shook her head. "It's not that big of a deal. I'm still doing well, but I was hoping to expand."

"Maybe you still can," he said, seeming distracted and she wondered where all that fierceness had gone.

"Maybe," she said, but she doubted it.

Silence like fog filled the car so completely she felt as though she had to squint across the center console just to see him. As it was, their stilted conversation was practically shouted over the sound of wind whistling through the canvas roof.

"What is one of the richest land developers on the East Coast doing driving a car like this?" she asked.

"What do you mean?" His lip quirked even as he tried to sound offended.

"I mean, were they out of Jaguars?"

He shrugged. "I don't need another car," he said. "This one still works."

"Yeah, but you could drive anything you want." She thought of her secret lust for a totally inappropriate Cooper Mini—with the racing stripes.

"I could, but—" He looked at her. Assessed. She suddenly realized that Jonah was going to reveal something about himself. He was actually going to open up and hand her a little Jonah nugget.

"Chicks dig the Jeep."

She tipped back her head and laughed. Oh, he was slick. The tension that had been coiling ever tighter in her since deciding to take the trip, relaxed.

"Mom taught me not to waste," he said when she stopped laughing. "And buying things I don't need always seemed pretty wasteful."

"You didn't have a lot growing up?" she asked, putting together the small pieces of him she did know.

He shook his head, but remained silent.

"We didn't, either," she said. "That's why Mom cleaned houses and took care—"

"Where was your dad?"

"He left when I was seven." She studied the familiar land outside her window. She hadn't wanted Jonah in her house because it would make this too personal and yet, here she was talking about the things she rarely talked about—to anyone.

No doubt he would be doing the math. Two men—a father and a husband—who had left her for greener pastures.

"I knew a lot of kids growing up whose parents got

divorced," he said. "And I watched what it did to those kids and I always thought I had it better."

Understanding dawned in her and those bands of intimacy she'd been trying to ignore or erase since realizing he wasn't the Dirty Developer, tightened. She felt every one of them. Heavy, thick bands of wanting him. Knowing him. And since she'd come to grips with wanting him, she was fine with those constraints. It was knowing this man, this practical stranger, as well as she felt she did that made her uncomfortable—that made the steam inside her hotter.

Nearly unbearable.

"Because you didn't have a dad?" she asked. "That's why it's better?"

His blue eyes were both warm and cold. Sympathetic and distant—the very contrary nature of Jonah.

"So I couldn't miss him when he was gone," he said.

Her stomach dipped and twisted in sudden sympathy for the hurt kid that still lived in Jonah.

Instead, she thought, her heart breaking for the guy, *you walk around pretending you never needed a dad.*

I don't want to know this about him, she thought desperately, even as she sucked up these crumbs of information like a Hoover.

She clenched her fists and tried to clear her mind of this stupid curiosity. This foolish compassion.

The landscape began to change. Fields gave way to homes, which gave way to apartments and stores. Grass was replaced by concrete. As they left her world behind, she felt herself get a grip and find the distance she needed to keep a cool head. She put the brakes on her heart's little meltdown and got her head back in the game.

They needed small talk. Chitchat. Empty banter. No more of this Dr. Phil stuff.

"Are you excited about tonight?" she asked, brightly.

"Good God, no."

"Really? An open bar, an almost guarantee of shrimp and, if we're lucky, some sushi—"

"You like sushi?"

"I am sushi's biggest fan."

"Well, then that part does sound good." His charm was unexpected and effective.

"Beautiful people will get drunk and do ridiculous things while wearing ridiculous clothes. Maybe—"

"I'm getting an award," he said, and she stared at him openmouthed.

"What kind?" she asked, wondering why he'd made receiving an award sound like getting a root canal.

"No idea," he answered, checking his mirrors and changing lanes on the four-lane highway.

"Well, are you excited about that?"

"Umm, no."

"There's nothing you're the slightest bit excited about?" She had a top-ten list of things she was thrilled over, not the least of which was seeing Jonah in a tux—then, hopefully, seeing him out of that tux.

"There is one thing," he said. When his eyes met hers, heat exploded in the Jeep.

"What's that?" she managed to squeak.

"I'm excited to see you," he murmured.

If he had uttered a blatant invitation, she might have laughed. But it wasn't. It was sexy and sincere and the combination almost blew her clothes right off. "In the dress. Having fun."

I'm excited to see you, too, she thought, her brain going X-rated on her.

Her instinct was to turn away, hiding a blush and pretending that this sexually loaded moment hadn't happened. But she fought that instinct and smiled at him, hoping it seemed confident, perhaps even seductive.

"Well, then," she said. "That makes two of us."

JONAH TUCKED his cell phone between his shoulder and ear and tried to slide his cuff link into place while waiting for Gary to pick up.

"It's Gary. Leave a message." It was the fourth time Jonah had heard that message in the past hour since he and Daphne had checked into their two-bedroom suite at the Waldorf Astoria.

"Gary," he said, tossing the silver cuff link onto the dresser. "Listen, call me back about that land. Did you make an offer without consulting me?" His headache rose up behind his eyes like the tide and he pinched the bridge of his nose. How could he have forgotten about that land? How could he have been so stupid? "We need to talk." He checked his watch.

Quarter to eight. The party started at seven-thirty and he was slated to get his award at nine. "I'm leaving for the gala, so I won't pick up but leave a message. It's important I know what we're doing about that land."

He hung up and flung his phone on the bed.

A conscience? Now? Because of Daphne?

He jabbed the cuff links through the holes on his white dress shirt. *What will I do if we have bought it? Rescind the offer? Sell some of the land to her?*

For a second he hung his head.

A month ago he wouldn't have even thought of these

things. A month ago he would have chalked up her palpable disappointment to the nature of business. And he would have still slept with her tonight.

That made him pause. Sex was where this was leading, there was no doubt. Despite her protestations at the school picnic, at some point since then, she'd changed her mind and had nearly jumped him on the way here.

That makes two of us.

And the invitation in her eyes had practically killed him. Christ. What a mess.

Not even checking to see if his tie was straight, he stalked across their shared living space to Daphne's shut door.

When had this gotten so complicated? It was supposed to be a business arrangement. A favor. A little quid pro quo on the escort front. Instead he now stood in front of her door, practically light-headed from the constant pooling of blood between his legs. Worse, he was dying to see her in that dress and was feeling like an ass for wanting her so bad when he might have just bought land right out from under her. Land he was going to build a hotel on so he could drive his father and brothers out of business.

I am such an asshole.

He lifted his hand to knock as the ebonized door slid soundlessly open over the thick burgundy carpet. What it revealed was something he never expected. Not in his wildest dreams.

For a second he couldn't breathe, and his hand remained aloft while his brain shot scattered impulses through his entire body.

Touch her.
Hold her.
Kiss her.

Don't go to the damn party.

"Jonah?" she asked, eyeing his hand with a sardonic smile.

She was stunning, bathed in the warm yellow light from the lamp behind her. But he'd been expecting that.

The red cocktail dress was structured, almost corseted and her breasts were right there, ripe and so white he wanted to make snow angels in her cleavage. Her blond hair was pulled back in some mysterious feminine knot that was held in place by silver chopsticks.

Her shoulders were strong and her arms toned.

The black gloves were an unexpected twist, hugging her wrists, her long fingers, the curve of her elbow. His mouth went dry at the erotic implications of those gloves. They were the sexiest thing he'd ever seen.

Although the long length of her legs ending in a pair of black stilettos was a close second.

And the combination of her body, her dress, those damn gloves and the knowing, powerful feminine glint in her eyes nearly brought him to his knees.

He was torn apart by her.

And she knew it.

He'd expected her to be beautiful. A butterfly emerging from a hardworking organic farmer cocoon.

But he hadn't expected her to own this beauty as much as she did.

"Shall we go?" she asked, picking up a small silver purse.

Numb, turned on, barely able to stand upright, he nodded and followed her.

IT WAS HARD WORK trying to keep Jonah from glowering at every person who approached him. It was hard work trying to keep him from frowning at the well-wishers, and taking off the heads of those people stupid enough to tell him that they always knew he "wasn't such a bastard after all."

The gloves helped. All Daphne had to do was raise a black finger to her chin, or if he really seemed off-put by some real estate agent's comment, she went so far as to press a finger to the top of her breasts, he would see it and his eyes would go a bit hazy and the glower would leave his face.

It was hard work but, dear Lord, it was fun.

She'd forgotten how fun it was to dress up. To do her hair and to put on makeup.

To wear silk stockings, lace underwear and not much else under a dress.

The high heels, however, while a crucial ingredient, were a huge pain.

But the gloves...oh, the gloves.

She got hot just thinking about what she wanted to do with these gloves and Jonah.

The ballroom at the Waldorf Astoria was filled with glitter: diamonds, chandeliers, blindingly white teeth. She was practically agog at the beautiful women walking by casting sideways glances at Jonah and then at her.

That's right, she wanted to tell them. *He's with me!*

But the most magnetic thing in the room was Jonah. The way he looked in a tux exceeded every expectation she had. The guy was built. Tall, strong. His shoulders wide. His hips narrow and the tux made him seem dangerous.

Her body had been humming the James Bond theme song all night.

The room smelled of wealth and business, sweetened slightly by the huge arrangements of stargazer lilies and what had to be gallons of Chanel Number 5 on the pulse points of at least half the women in the room.

A waiter walked by and Daphne grabbed two glasses of champagne, pressing one into Jonah's hand.

"To Cinderella," she said, clinking her glass to his and taking a sip. Oh, her whole body shivered. That champagne was the real deal.

The glittering crowd parted and over Jonah's shoulder she glimpsed a regal blonde wearing a silver dress that fell like water over every curve from shoulder to floor.

"Wow," Daphne whispered and Jonah glanced behind him.

"Hey, look," Jonah said, grabbing her elbow and turning her a hundred and eighty degrees away from the silver water goddess. "Sushi. I'll introduce you as long as you don't go all biggest fan on it."

"Who is that woman?" she asked, allowing herself be led away with a backward glance. "And why are you so mad at these people? Don't you work with them?" She drained the last of the champagne, feeling it go right to her knees in the best possible way.

"These people are pests and she's the worst," he said, loading up a plate with sushi from the elaborate ice sculpture buffet.

Sushi and shrimp and oysters.

It was heaven.

"So why are you here?" she asked, making sure he got enough of the salmon roll. "If you don't like all these people."

"A means to an end," he said. "They sell me land, then they sell my condos. Don't get me wrong, there are a lot of people here tonight who I like. But I would never be invited and I would never be getting an award if it didn't make them look better for doing it."

"That's awfully cynical," she said, grabbing another plate because he'd ignored the oysters totally.

He paused for a moment. "That's me," he said. And it wasn't a joke. He was telling her, letting her know, yet again, not to be fooled.

She shrugged. "Sucks to be you," she quipped.

"Well, well, if it isn't our Dirty Developer come Environmental Bastion." The woman in silver appeared at Jonah's side. Her face was utterly composed, as if she were carved of ice—or maybe Botox—but her eyes practically drank him in.

Jonah tensed. As much as the woman was sending him a good-to-go message, Jonah apparently was having none of it. The air between them blew cold.

"Hello, Tina," he said, his lips barely moving. Tina didn't seem to notice Jonah's vibe and she threw Daphne a blatantly calculating glance.

If Tina thought she could make off with Daphne's date—especially when said date clearly had no interest—then she had another think coming.

Sorry to set down her plate, Daphne bid a mental adieu to the oysters and put her hand on Jonah's arm, leaning in close as though she'd been resting her breasts against Jonah's body most of her days.

Jonah's hand quickly covered hers and squeezed.

"I'm Daphne Larson," she said, holding out the hand that wasn't occupied with Jonah.

"Tina," the woman replied with a cold fish handshake. And went back to giving Jonah her unwanted attention. "Interesting press release from your company on Friday."

"Well," he said, not smiling, "I'm glad we could entertain."

As cold as he seemed, Jonah began to stroke Daphne's fingers, and the sensation was both muted and amplified by the material. Ripples spread out from her fingers to her arms, across her shoulders, down her chest to her breasts and farther.

She fought not to gasp. Good Lord, he was seducing her in front of a ballroom of people.

"Your Haven House charity sounds fascinating," Tina said, clearly unaware that Daphne was about to pass out from lust. "We should set up a meeting so we can discuss how my office can best help you."

"Haven House, which is not in any kind of planning stages, will not be in New York City," he said, pressing his thumb into the soft center of Daphne's palm.

Oh sweet heaven. She knew she should be following this conversation. Jonah had a charity? Haven House? What—

He linked their fingers, holding her tightly, palm to palm, nothing but satin between them.

Daphne swallowed a little groan.

Tina shrugged. "As your clientele would surely be from the city, I think our interest is understandable."

"Tina." Jonah's lips curved in a smile so chilling Daphne felt it cut into her overheated state. "You can drop the game. You're not interested in the charity. Stop wasting your time."

Daphne had to hand it to the woman—she didn't blanche, she didn't turn red, she didn't even smack Jonah. She laughed. And flicked a glare to Daphne from those diamond-hard eyes. But there was something a bit sad in those depths. Something a little lost.

"Good luck with him, honey," Tina said. "Wear the gloves tonight so you don't lose fingers to frostbite."

Then she left. The view of her gown from the back was as stunning as it had been from the front. People made way for her, as if realizing she was a force to be reckoned with.

"Who was that?" Daphne tried to pretend she was totally together.

"Tina Schneider. She's married to the deputy mayor of New York."

Daphne laughed. "Does she know that?"

"We used to date a million years ago."

Oh. Of course.

She grabbed another glass of champagne and downed it, a little bit of the magic in the evening leeching away.

"Have I told you you are beautiful?" he asked and the champagne raced to her head, with a dose of arousal not far behind.

"Not—" She sucked in a breath when he lifted her palm to his lips and kissed it. The wet heat of his breath burned through the silk. "Exactly."

"You are," he answered. His eyes practically drilling her to the ice sculpture. "You are the most beautiful woman in this room."

Ex-girlfriend who? What?

He released her hand and she brought it to her own lips, to feel the lingering warmth. His eyes flashed as he watched. She touched her bottom lip with her fingers, let her hand rest slightly against the white skin of her neck and smiled, channeling a little Mae West.

"You're not so bad yourself," she said.

He leaned toward her, clearly about to kiss her. She was more than ready to be kissed.

The P.A. system buzzed to life and a short, balding man stepped onto the curtained dais at the far end of the ballroom. He blinked owlishly against the bright spotlight that found him at the podium.

"Good evening, everyone," he said. "And welcome to the annual tristate real estate gala."

There was a spattering of polite applause and the moment between Daphne and Jonah shattered. Jonah smiled ruefully and his gaze lingered at her lips before he turned to the high cocktail table where they'd placed their plates earlier.

"Let's eat while they talk," he said.

Daphne's breath hitched. She needed a second to get herself together. She simply wasn't used to near kisses, and deputy mayor's wives, champagne and black satin gloves. Her head was swimming.

"When do you get your award?"

He checked his watch. "About ten minutes."

"I'll be right back," she said and made her way to the nearest women's restroom.

It was cool in the bathroom, and when the door shut behind her, Daphne felt as if she was in a quiet cocoon.

A very fancy cocoon.

Even this room had a chandelier and stargazer lilies in sterling silver vases. She collapsed into one of the white Queen Anne chairs in front of the mirror and tipped her head against the back and closed her eyes.

"In over your head with him, aren't you?" a cool voice asked.

Daphne opened her eyes to see Tina looking just as elegant upside down.

"Ah, pardon?" Daphne asked, straightening and opening her purse to search for her two-year-old, drugstore lip gloss. Anything to seem occupied. Anything to not have this conversation.

"Jonah." Tina sat next to her, opened her purse and removed a tube of Chanel lipstick.

Of course.

"We're friends."

Tina smiled and it sliced the air between them like a dagger. "That's what he tells all the women he sleeps with. So when it goes bad, he can shrug and say, 'I told you we were just friends.'"

This was a classic woman-scorned situation. Daphne felt for Tina, she really did, but she wasn't going to let this ruin her night.

"Maybe all those girls Jonah slept with before didn't listen," Daphne said, standing, lip gloss forgotten. "Maybe they thought they could change him."

"You don't?" Tina asked, clearly not believing her.

"Good God, no," Daphne said, laughing. People didn't change for other people, at least not permanently. If Jonah was to become a different kind of man, he'd have to do it for himself.

Tina sneered, and Daphne wondered what Jonah saw in this angry woman. Or maybe it was Jonah who made her so angry and that made her sad for all of them.

"Go on believing that," Tina said, "if it helps. But be warned, that guy will break your heart."

Daphne caught Tina's reflection in yet another mirror, as the woman slowly put on lipstick—thin, glamorous, wealthy and not a speck of dirt under her fingernails. Yet Daphne walked out of there glad not to have to trade places.

She was glad she wasn't in danger of being hurt by Jonah. That she saw him for what he was.

A one-night Prince Charming.

JONAH STOOD where she'd left him, fresh plates of food beside him on the table. Seeing him by himself while surrounded by people, she was struck full in the chest by a pang of longing.

It wasn't just because he was so handsome. And it wasn't because he'd made it obvious that he found her equally attractive.

He seemed so alone in the midst of all of those people who had no idea who he was. So in need of a friend.

And just like that she recognized what Tina had meant. It wasn't that those women didn't listen to Jonah, when he said they were just friends. It was that Jonah never meant it. Not really. He didn't have friends. Probably didn't know how to make that type of relationship work.

Daphne pressed a hand to her stomach, feeling sympathy and respect for him that she knew she shouldn't. Those emotions would make the end of this charade more painful than it needed to be.

He grabbed two champagne flutes from a passing waiter as he saw her.

And smiled. An intimate but honest smile. I'm glad to see you, that smile said. I'm glad you're here.

Ah, crap, she thought.

Her heart, which she'd been so sure was out of reach, unbreakable, told her to run. To get while the getting was good.

But the rest of her body vetoed the idea. On trembling legs she crossed the navy and tan carpet to be at his side.

"I had to fight ten men to get all these oysters so you better eat up," he told her when she was within whispering distance.

She eyed the plates and eyed her black satin gloves,

wondering how—back in the day—women ate anything without destroying a pair of gloves a night.

"Just take one off," Jonah whispered in her ear, his breath toying with the fine hair at her nape. "No one will know."

Not wasting another second, Daphne pulled off one glove, revealing her work-roughened hands, and polished off six oysters, a plate of shrimp and a few of the best tuna rolls she'd ever had.

In fact, she was so enthralled by the spicy tuna she almost didn't hear the speaker begin to introduce Jonah.

"He's done more for the environment in the tristate area than any one developer," the balding man said. He was red under the spotlight, his forehead shining with sweat. "To say nothing of the fact that he's made several agents in this room very, very wealthy."

A few people laughed but mostly, people turned and stared at Jonah. Whispers started up behind hands and his back straightened. His jaw got so tight Daphne worried about his molars.

"In light of his new charity, Haven House, the Organization for Tristate Realtors would like to present Jonah Closky with a donation to Haven House of fifty thousand dollars."

The room rang with applause and Daphne nearly choked on a tuna roll. That was a lot of money. Especially considering these people didn't seem to like him, and he positively didn't like them.

The applause went on. And on. The speaker, now holding a giant check, coughed uncomfortably and it broadcasted through the whole room.

"Jonah?" she whispered. "You have to—" She stopped. He knew what he had to do, he just didn't want to do it. It was written in every hard line on his face. Every clenched muscle.

He was going to cut off his nose to spite his face.

And she wasn't done with her oysters.

I COULD WALK OUT, Jonah thought, liking the idea. Meanwhile the people around him stopped smiling and the claps in the corners of the room began to die off.

Some of these people had tried to rob him. All of them had bad-mouthed him, whispered malicious things about Gary and him and what they were trying to do. A few people had gone so far as to try to sabotage him.

None of them knew him. And now all of them would want something from him, and, because of the money, he'd be obligated to listen. To pretend. To join in the falseness of it all.

His skin literally crawled at the thought.

He could leave. They could take their money and—

Daphne's hand, naked and warm, slid into his and squeezed until he looked at her.

Her big green eyes were wide and wise. "Sometimes, Jonah," she said, "you have to let love in. Even when it hurts."

"It's not real," he whispered to her, appalled that she would mistake this political posturing for something honest or genuine.

"The money is," she said giving his hand a good shake. "And that's enough from these people."

The woman was right.

He squeezed her hand and headed for the stage, for that big check and the false sentiment. He concentrated on the good that money would do and on Daphne.

Daphne who was turning out to be the biggest surprise of them all.

CHAPTER TWELVE

SHE'D HAD FOUR glasses of champagne. *Four.* Was Daphne drunk? Jonah didn't think so. She walked a straight line. Didn't slur her words.

Feeling a little guilty, are we? Jonah's conscience, asleep for the past fifteen years, had been talking his ear off most of the night. *Thinking you want to take advantage of a woman you're already screwing thanks to that land purchase? A woman who might just be a little drunk?*

I am scum, he thought.

"That—" Daphne sighed as the doors slid closed and the elevator jumped slightly before sending them upward "—was a lot of fun."

He tried not to look at her, because frankly, looking at her was turning into foreplay. She was doing wicked things with those gloves and his internal engine had been running hot all night.

But in the end he couldn't resist a glance. She was standing in the corner, braced slightly against the gold handrails. Her reflection doubled over and over in the mirrored walls.

"I'm glad you had a good time," he said.

She eyed him shrewdly. "Did you have fun?"

He could lie, stay on his side of the elevator and watch

the numbers illuminate over the doors. Or, he could tell her the truth. He could look her in the eye and say, *Yes, I had fun. I had fun looking at you and those wicked gloves and that tight dress. In fact, I had so much fun my pants don't fit right.*

Well, he clearly wasn't going to say all that.

So he simply nodded and the elevator still nearly burst into flames.

"Jonah," she said, her voice tugging him free from his thoughts. She no longer smiled like Mae West. Instead it was just Daphne there. Daphne who'd known he wasn't what the whole world thought he was before she even had proof. Daphne who'd rushed to his defense. Stood by his side. Who'd told him she *didn't do this kind of thing,* the last time they'd been in this position.

He shifted sideways, boxing her in slightly and her breasts rose with a hard breath. Her eyes dilated.

It was time to get to the bottom of this.

"Daphne—"

The elevator pinged and the doors slid open.

Jonah, frustrated, grabbed her hand and pulled her into the hallway toward their room. He jerked the key card into the reader then threw open the door. Holding it for her, he caught the surprising green grass scent of her as she passed and his frustration built. His blood beat hard.

"Daphne," he said when the door closed behind them, leaving them in a dark cocoon, lit only by the city lights outside their windows. The whole world glittered and it was reflected in her wide eyes.

"Jonah," she said, facing him. Her face was a perfect canvas for the glow from the city. She was made more stunning, more mysterious in the shadows and light.

"You told me last week that you couldn't do—" he lifted

a hand, waved it between them to indicate all the teasing, the pounding blood, the long looks, the smell of sex that practically rolled off them "—this."

"I know," she whispered.

"I am ready to respect that and say good night—"

"No!" She surprised both of them with her vehemence. "I don't want that."

Ah, the window of opportunity beckoned.

"What do you want?" he asked, slowly advancing on her. He tossed the key on the floor. Her purse fell from limp fingers.

"I want—" She paused and he kept advancing, stalking her practically. She took another deep breath, those breasts, those marvelous breasts trembling in the gilded shadows. "You."

He'd expected it, had practically fed her the line. But like the way she looked tonight, he wasn't ready for the impact.

Every other woman who said that to him—and there had been plenty—had uttered the words because it was something sexy to say. They'd been talking about his body. His dick. His money. Hell, who knows what else, because they certainly hadn't been talking about him.

But Daphne knew him better than any woman he'd ever slept with. And still she wanted *him*. Jonah Closky.

It stopped him in his tracks.

She blinked at him as the silence between them stretched and he struggled to shut up his conscience while remembering the steps to this particular dance. But she'd stripped away what was familiar and left him feeling naked. And young.

"Okay," she finally said, brightly as if she were suddenly wrangling kindergartners. "We've got that settled. So, maybe if we could—"

"Are you trying to organize this?" he asked, smiling incredulously. Ah, Daphne. Only she could make him want to laugh in this particular scenario.

"No," she said, then winced. "Well, maybe. I'm a bit…rusty."

The hum in his blood intensified and he took those few long steps necessary to stand right in front of her. He felt the heat of her along his chest, his legs. She tilted her face up and he could smell the sweet champagne on her breath.

"I want this Jonah," she whispered. "I really do."

"Good," he said. "So do I."

Warmth flared in those green eyes. Her hands, clad in those unbelievable black gloves, stroked the center of his chest, from tie to belt and back again.

All the while her eyes bored into his, searching out his secrets.

His fingers traced her collarbone, ran its delicate length until he found the hard pounding of her blood in her throat. He bent his head and kissed her there, sucked her flesh into his mouth and when she groaned, straining against him, he pulled her into his arms and bit her. Just a little.

"Oh my." She sighed.

He felt her kick off her shoes then she went after his jacket, then his belt. His tie was yanked off and suddenly he didn't have a shirt on. He let her strip him because he was far too preoccupied by the trembling tops of breasts, pushed up so dramatically by her dress. He couldn't stop running his hands along the boning at her waist.

It was all so delicious.

But then she started to pull off her gloves and he had to stop her.

"No," he said.

"No what?" she gasped.

"Leave the gloves on." He smiled, the surge of lust hitting a new height.

"Okay," she whispered. He touched her hands, her waist. Cupped the flesh of her breasts through the dress and she bit her lip as if to stem a cry.

Then, as he had wanted to do from nearly the moment he saw her, he let down her hair.

The chopsticks fell to the thick carpet as she sighed and lifted her gloved hands to her head to shake out thick curtains of nearly white blond hair. It fell past her shoulders almost to the center of her back and it was everything he'd thought it would be.

He reached his fingers into the silky depths, fanned it out over her beautiful shoulders.

"You're so beautiful," he said, and she blushed. The colors of Daphne—white, red, pink and black—were so dramatic and erotic he could barely stand it.

"So are you," she said, running a finger over his chest, down this stomach to the waistband of his pants.

She ducked her head and he brushed back some of the hair that fell forward just in time to see her bite her lower lip before sliding that hand over the fly of his pants to press against his erection.

He sucked in as much air as he could and it still wasn't enough. His heart pounded so hard his hands shook. To keep himself steady he pressed her hard against the nearest wall, lifting her slightly, so when his body came to rest against hers, it rested in all the right spots.

"Yes," she hissed, digging those gloves into his hair, over his neck, holding on tight to his shoulders.

Pressing fevered kisses to her neck and breasts, he found

the small zipper at her waist. Leaning back, so he could see what was unwrapped, he pulled the zipper down her body and the dress loosened, gaped and finally fell in a red silk puddle at her feet.

He opened his mouth, ready with a compliment but his brain went blank at the sight of her. The heat coursing through his body welded his tongue to the roof of his mouth and he was speechless.

This…this body and the lace and the satin had all been hidden under that dress. He was never going to be able to look at her the same way again. The next time he saw her wearing mud-splattered jeans he was going to imagine this moment and he'd fall to the ground at her feet in thanks.

Her laugh, empowered and feminine and hot, made him lift his eyes to hers.

"That look is the best compliment I've had in years," she said, running her hands along her sides, around her waist and then, her gaze still engaged with his, she ran those gloves up to her breasts. Her nipples peeking out from the blond hair and black satin.

Her eyes were as naked as her body and he could see himself in them. A reflection that he didn't recognize, colored all wrong by her feelings for him. Feelings he knew were perilously close to love.

Oh, Daphne, he thought. *Don't feel this way. Don't hurt yourself on me.*

Tenderness and this sneaky regret weren't wanted at this moment, they certainly weren't what the beauty in his arms wanted as she arched against the wall, her body vibrating so much he could hear it.

He growled low in his throat and turned her around so she faced the wall. So he couldn't see himself and all those things she shouldn't be feeling in her eyes. Pressing his chest to the cool skin of her back, they both groaned. He cupped her hips, followed the lace edge of her underwear around to the front and ran his finger along the hot center seam of her body.

She arched against him, her bottom against his erection and he pushed away her hair to expose her neck. In the morning she'd be marked and the thought made him even hotter.

Daphne braced her hands against the wall and he felt the lace under his fingers grow wet.

"I'm so ready for you," he growled in her ear, and she whimpered, tucking her head against him, her hips pulsing against his hands. "You feel ready for me."

"I am." She panted and swore and he smiled, feeling feral. Raw and wild.

Using his free hand, he dug out his wallet and the condom he had there. Not breaking stride with his fingers he undid his pants and kicked free of them.

"I need a second," he said and she cried out, grabbing his hand when he would have pulled away. "A second," he murmured, nipping her neck.

She let him go and he grabbed the waist of her lace panties and pulled them over her hips, down to her ankles. He rolled the condom on, straightened, then inserted one leg between hers.

"Spread your legs, Daphne."

"What?" she whispered.

"Your legs, baby. Let me in."

She shifted, the smell of her arousal intensified and he bent his legs, positioned himself at her entrance and in one smooth, hard thrust pushed himself all the way home.

Daphne came immediately, as if she'd been waiting for him to do this all night. It took every once of control he had not to follow her right over the edge. She was so hot and sweet in his arms, crying his name and shaking. And it seemed to Jonah, at that moment, that this was different.

This wasn't just sex.

And he was way out of his league.

DAPHNE STARED at Jonah.

Pulling the million-thread-count sheets around herself, she sat up and stared at him while he pretended to sleep. "Open your eyes, you big faker," she said.

And he smiled, his face relaxed and handsome under his rumpled hair. She wanted to avert her eyes, as if by not looking at him she could somehow repair the damage that had already been done. But it was too late. Even if she were blind, she'd be mostly in love with Jonah Closky.

Her body hurt, ached, pulsed and throbbed in places she'd thought were ghost towns. But her heart…her heart was singing.

"You know what will happen if I open my eyes," he mumbled, still smiling. And her heart sang louder, deafening her to the screams of her common sense.

"Come on, I've taken them off," she said, knowing what he referred to.

His eyes snapped open in horror. "You didn't."

She waved her naked hands at him. "You pretty much ruined them with that last trick of yours."

Sighing, he leaned up to kiss her shoulder. "We'll have to get you a new pair." He rearranged himself on the bed, so he rested against the headboard, the sheet pooling in his lap.

Moonlight crept through the room, leaving sharp slices of shadows in the corners and across one side of the bed.

But Jonah sat in a shard of white light, his body like stone, smooth and hard. The light played tricks on her perspective. He was here, so close she could count his eyelashes, see the scar at the corner of his eye that he'd said was from chicken pox, yet he seemed so far away. The shadows added distance where there wasn't any.

Daphne, because she couldn't help it, because he was here right now and tomorrow night he wouldn't be, ran her hands down the muscled hairless expanse of his chest, over the slight ridges at his stomach. She hooked a thumb in the sheet and he caught her hand, laughing.

"Baby, even if we still had those gloves, four times in a night is beyond me."

She wrinkled her nose, eager to hoard him, stock up so when she went back into her long hibernation she'd have enough memories to survive. She'd had a night like she'd never had—a sexual experience so rich and erotic she couldn't believe she'd been the one against the wall, or in the shower or all over this bed.

But it was her. And she couldn't be happier.

She patted the lump under the sheet and smiled, removing her hands. "Can I ask you something?"

"Sure," he said, grinning expansively. "As long as it isn't what you asked me while we—"

"Stop!" she cried, covering his mouth with her hands, embarrassed by those things she'd done in the heat of sex. "Don't."

He laughed, kissing her hands before pulling them down. "What's your question?"

Cradling his face, she sighed, wondering if this would

end the night. End them. But she figured she'd never be in a place to get a more honest answer from him. And while he'd be gone from her life at some point, the Mitchells would be around forever.

She stroked his shoulders and, before she even said the words, he tensed as if waiting for them. "Why are you so mad at Patrick?"

WHY AM I SO MAD at Patrick? Jonah thought, turning the words over and over as though they were foreign and he couldn't quite make out the translation between what he felt—the cold pit in his stomach reserved for Patrick Mitchell—and the word *mad.*

For some reason, sitting in this bed with Daphne, Jonah remembered being nine, after recovering from the chicken pox, when Sheila took him to the pool. Jonah would sit on the bottom underwater, looking up at the silver disk of the sun and the above-water world shimmering over his head. He'd hold his breath until he thought his lungs would burst, then he'd push off, reaching for that silver disk, and explode out of the water with a pop and gasp.

He looked at Daphne, thought about the Mitchells and his mother and held his breath. But he knew it was futile. Daphne was the glittering disk and he was running out of air.

But still, stubborn and hardheaded, he held on until the last minute.

"It's complicated," he told her, pulling her hands from his shoulders and holding them tightly in his.

"Then explain it to me," she urged, ducking her head to try to maintain eye contact.

He felt his whole body flinch. "Explain?" he asked and she nodded.

Like it's that easy? he wanted to say. But he looked at her and realized that it actually was.

He wanted to tell her. This woman. Because she was so good. So decent and beautiful. So vulnerable and strong.

But it wasn't easy, and the words cost him something, like taking out a chunk of his chest or a slice from his belly.

This, he thought, feeling acidic and grumpy, *is why I don't explain things.*

But nonetheless, he looked deep in her sympathetic green eyes and pushed off the bottom of the pool.

"It's not Patrick," he said, his voice gruff, the words rising up rusty and thick. "Well, not totally. It's my mom."

He watched his thumb trace the hills and valleys of her hand and felt her breathe. He could smell them, both of them, and the sex they'd had rise up out of the soft sheets.

And he'd never felt closer to another person before in his life. Something like lust, something like joy filled him, bringing his head up.

This was intimacy. Those things they'd done to each other, the places they'd touched—that was sex. This was something different, a potent mix of friendship and camaraderie.

And he'd never had this with any other woman. With another person.

"I know everyone thinks it's because I'm so hurt by the fact that he wasn't around for my childhood, and that's part of it." The things he'd never verbalized fell out of his mouth and it was easy. It was welcome. "But when I was a kid my mom asked me if I wanted to know my dad. She said she would write Patrick and tell him about me, but I said no. And as the years went on I felt bad about stopping her from talking to Patrick. Not for me, but for her." He looked at Daphne to see if any of this was registering. "She always loved him, it was obvious even to me, and I thought I was keeping them apart. But as I got older I realized it wasn't me—it was him. Patrick with his silence rejected her over and over again."

Daphne squeezed his hand and he realized he'd stopped tracing her palm and was instead gripping her like a lifeline when he was about to drown.

"But she's here now. I mean, they're in the same place and she still loves him and he's looking at her like he never told her to stay away. Like the thirty years they spent apart never happened. I know she hasn't told him what it was like for us—she's so proud. But I think what's holding her back from trying to have a second chance with Patrick is me. Me and my vocal, childish disapproval of him—"

"Oh, Jonah." Daphne sighed and he realized that she got it. She understood and he so appreciated her, he leaned over and kissed her delicately on the cheek.

"I can tell that if I let this go, if I—" he took a big breath "—admit that this guy is my dad and Gabe and Max are my brothers, then there will be nothing keeping them apart. Nothing to stop her from trying to be a wife to him."

"What's wrong with that?" she asked. "If that's what they both want?"

"He'll hurt her," he cried, wondering what had happened to her understanding. "All over again. And I don't think she could take it. She spent her whole life missing him. Thinking less of herself for things she couldn't control. And I know if I go back to the inn and call that man *Dad*, then she'll forget about those letters. She'll forget about those hard years and she'll take whatever second chance he gives her."

"He's a good man, Jonah. There would be worse things in the world."

Daphne should know better, he thought, feeling his face harden.

"I don't have to tell you, Daphne," he said, not wanting to be cruel, but wanting so badly to get his point across, "that nice people don't always get it right. I'm sure Jake didn't want to hurt you."

She sucked in a breath, the fine muscles of her lips twitching, and he touched them, wanting to take away the hurt he'd caused.

"You're right," she said. "There is no guarantee. What if she and Patrick get back together anyway? They're adults, Jonah. You can't stop them from doing what they want."

"I can try," he said, shaking his head. "She's my mother and I have to try to protect her."

"You're a good son," Daphne said, wrapping her hand around his neck and squeezing, pressing her soft face to his.

"I never want her to feel like she's less of a woman or a mother because that man rejects her again."

"Maybe he won't reject her," Daphne said. "From what Gabe and Max have said, it's like he's been waiting for her all these years."

"Then he shouldn't have sent those letters. He shouldn't have told her to stay away."

Daphne pulled back and steadied him as if reading him. "For a man with so much pride I thought you'd understand it a bit better when you see it in your father."

He wanted to reject her assessment, but he'd seen it enough to agree. He and Patrick were a lot alike. He didn't want to bring this fight into the bed. Not on his one night with Daphne.

Not when there were other things they could do.

So he smiled and touched the veil of hair that fell over her shoulder, carefully spread his fingers so long strands of it fell into his palm. "You're right," he said. "And the truth is I see a lot of myself in those men. I actually like Max and Gabe." He shrugged. "Sort of. But I can't risk it with Patrick."

She pressed a kiss to his mouth. Nothing sexy or leading, just a kiss. Warm and soft. Her lips against his. And he kissed her back.

Something had short-circuited his brain. Instead of being uncomfortable by all they had talked about, and all that he'd revealed, he found himself charged with a certain electricity. An energy.

"Any more questions?" he asked, looking at her lips, then her breasts covered by the sheet.

"What's Haven House?"

He laughed. "Give an inch, you'll take a mile."

She blushed and shrugged, his forthright Daphne. "You offered."

"It's a charity I'm starting with my business partner," he said, still stroking her hair, carefully working out some of the knots he'd put in it. He could talk all night as long as he could touch her while he did it. Not that he really wanted to talk, but he found himself in the bizarre place of wanting to make Daphne happy. So, he broke his rules again. And explained Haven House.

"When I was growing up, my mom had to work so hard she didn't have a chance to go back to school or learn skills that would help her get a better job. I know that's something that a lot of single mothers deal with."

"My mom did," she said.

He nodded. "So, hopefully someday we will be able to build a school and a residence and we'll offer scholarships so mothers can bring their kids for two weeks and both the mother and the kid can learn new skills. Skills that will hopefully add something to their lives that they didn't have before. And not just computers but art classes and maybe some writing classes. And the kids can learn how to play sports or—" He cut himself off, realizing he'd crossed the line between explaining and waxing poetic. "I get a little excited about the idea. Gary jumped the gun a bit with that press release. Right now it's nothing more than an idea."

"It's a great idea," she said, her voice betraying her emotion, and he saw tears in her eyes.

"Oh, no," he said, laughing, but uncomfortable. "No tears. Not in my bed. If you want to cry, you have to go back to your own room."

"Do you want me to?" she asked, serious, careful.

"What?"

"Go back to my room?"

"God, no," he said. It was the last thing he wanted. Tears or no, he wanted to keep her in his bed for a week. A month. As long as they could live on room service. So, he pulled the sheet free from her hands, revealing the breasts he'd been lavishing with X-rated attention.

"I thought you said you couldn't do four," she said, leaning back on her elbows, the trace of tears gone. Thank God.

"That," he said, "was before I met you." And then he jerked her legs around so he was between them. Just rough enough, just wild enough so her blood immediately rose to the challenge.

He lifted himself over her, hard and heavy against her thigh.

"How do you know what I need?" she asked, staring into his eyes. He could see right to her soul, her generous heart that she had on display.

Lie, his instincts told him. *Make a joke. Don't give yourself away.*

But he couldn't. Not to her. He stared in her eyes and let her see his own heart, battered and guarded, callused and crippled.

"Because it's what I need, too."

CHAPTER THIRTEEN

DAPHNE HAD EXPECTED awkward. She'd expected the worst kind of morning, followed by an even worse drive home, followed by a disaster of a goodbye scene when he dropped her off at the farm.

What she got was loving. Kind. Breakfast in bed. Joking conversations about school lunches and who had it worse growing up.

He's good at this, she thought at one point, staring at him on the sly. *He's had more than his share of morning afters.* His charm was in full force, never giving her a moment to get serious. To ask what happened next.

And finally, at the driver-side window of his Jeep, she got a kiss goodbye.

"I'll see you tomorrow morning," he said. The look in his eye, as if he knew all of her filthiest secrets—which he did—made her blush.

"Eight o'clock," she agreed, the usual time for her to either drop off the truck or go with him to deliver the lunches.

When are you leaving?

Why are we pretending?

How does this end?

Those questions were beating against her lips, screaming to get out and run amuck. But she harnessed them, muzzled them, and for once in her life, she just let things happen.

"Bye," she said, and ducked into the open window for one more kiss to his already kiss-swollen lips.

"Ouch," he muttered as he pulled back, touching the puffy bottom lip. "Somebody bit me last night," he joked, smiling just for her.

"Kiss me," she said, shocking herself, "or I'll do it again."

He kissed her like a man returning home from a long trip, like a man about to leave for a long trip. He kissed her like he couldn't stand any time apart from her.

And she was afraid she kissed him back the same way. How could he not taste the truth in that kiss?

Finally he drove away and she watched the Jeep kick up dust on its way down from her mountain.

"You're going to break my heart," she whispered, seeing the future as clearly as if it were happening now.

Wind blew up from the valley and she felt so hollow, suddenly. Her arms and legs weightless, her chest empty, she wondered if she'd blow away on a good strong gust.

"Daph?"

Daphne whirled to find her mother, a respectful distance away, but close enough that she would have seen everything.

"Mom," she groaned, "don't go getting yourself worked up. It's nothing permanent."

Gloria stood there, the cardigan she'd worn every cool morning since Daphne was a girl, wrapped snug around her waist. The elbows were threadbare, the red color now a dull brandy, faded from the years and hard use.

Gloria's face was inscrutable, the lines and wrinkles around her eyes and thinning lips gave away nothing. And something about Mom's stoicism made Daphne shake.

She clenched her hands together but the trembling traveled up her arms, across her shoulders and settled in her chest.

"I'm serious, Mom. He's going to leave." Her breath hitched as she said the word. "There will be no wedding, no babies." *Oh my God,* she could barely get that word out. And why was she crying? Why was this terrible pressure burning her chest, making it so hard to breathe?

"Sweetie," Mom cooed and wrapped Daphne up tight in her arms. The sweater, so ugly and old, felt like velvet against Daphne's face and she burrowed in tight. "You love him, don't you?"

The words were buried somewhere deep, somewhere scared and black and ugly. So she just nodded.

"Does he love you?"

"Of course not," she said, stunned by the thought. He lived so far away, occupied another stratosphere, a different planet.

Her mother's soft laughter stirred her hair. "Do you know that for sure?"

"Mom, it's stupid to even have this conversation," Daphne mumbled, putting her head back down on Mom's shoulder.

Gloria rested her chin on Daphne's head and rocked her ever so perfectly from side to side. "You know, sweetie, I hate to point this out to you when you're obviously ready to martyr yourself, but you've always been very good at loving people. You just have a hard time letting them love you back."

Daphne squeezed her eyes shut and gave herself one more moment of self-pity. Then she gathered herself up by the very fibers of her muscles, the sheer will she lived on day to day, and stepped away from her mother.

"How is Helen?" she said, wiping her tears, pushing her night with Jonah into memory and away from her reality.

"Don't you want to talk about this?" Mom asked, sympathy breathing from her pores, radiating from her sweater.

"No," Daphne said firmly. "I don't."

She was home now. Cinderella had had her night at the ball and now there was work to do.

ON HIS THREE HUNDREDTH call to Gary to find out about the land Jonah got a connection for about ten seconds.

"Gary," he whispered, standing on the hill behind the Riverview kitchen where he could see anyone coming. He didn't need eavesdroppers to this particular conversation.

"Jonah, our phones are going nuts! When are you coming back?"

"Back?"

"To work? Remember? I know you said you'd be gone until next week, but I need you as soon as you can get here. We've got Haven House donations coming in from every direction. The deputy mayor wants to talk to us about funding. Every major newspaper including *USA Today* wants an interview. We need you back here."

Back there.

He looked at the mountains, purple in the twilight, and something in him, something raw and new and unknown, howled *no*.

"I need another week here."

"Still?" Gary cried. "Hey, wait, I'm going to lose you for a second, I'm going in a tunnel."

Tunnel, Jonah thought. *He must be heading into the city.*

Jonah rubbed his forehead. And considered his reality, which, for the last little while, he'd been neglecting. He had work to do. Serious work. Hard work. Work that he loved and was important to him.

Here, he had his mother, who was acting like a stranger. And Daphne.

His whole body contracted at the thought of her. The thought of not seeing her again.

He shook his head. It was obviously time to go home if he was having such reactions. It was time to end this relationship before he got more stupid.

It had been a spectacular night, there was no doubt about it. But it didn't change the fact that he had to leave. There was no future for them.

The phone buzzed. "…Sorry. How was the gala?" Gary asked.

"Fine," Jonah said, which really didn't even cover a one-hundredth of the night. In fact, *fine* covered the food. That was it. The rest of the night was something reserved for the most explicit male fantasy. "But I'm calling to find out if we bought that land."

There was a long pause. "Gary?"

Static in the general tone of Gary's voice buzzed over his phone. "…stupid buildings. Sorry. What?"

"The land?" Jonah said, cursing Gary's crappy phone reception. "Did we buy it?"

"…no land—"

The line went dead.

"Gary?" There was no answer.

Relief flooded him and he tipped back his head to look up at the stars and he smiled. Thank God. It had bothered him every time they'd come up for air during the night— obviously not enough to sleep in the other room. But now that he knew he didn't have anything to feel guilty about he felt like laughing.

Last night had been amazing. And he didn't want

anything to sully the memory of it—since memories were all he was going to have of Daphne.

And, now, in the cold evening, away from Daphne's hot touch, he had their relationship back in perspective. It had been amazing and it had been a one-time thing.

Her life was here. His life couldn't be.

The inn, the Mitchells…even if he was interested in being a part of this family, he couldn't do it. Not if it meant putting his mother in the path of the man who hurt her so badly. Not if it meant risking all that he and Mom had managed to do— alone, without Gabe, Max and especially without Patrick.

A week, he thought. A week to tie up all his loose ends.

One more week with Daphne; the very thought was bittersweet.

He looked out at the cabins. Cabin four had a small light on, a beacon in the dark night.

Tying up loose ends. *Beginning,* he thought, *with Mom.*

PATRICK HAD BROUGHT a Scrabble game with him when he went to Iris's cabin. He'd tucked the aging red box under his arm for two reasons: one, she loved the game—they'd had all-night Scrabble tournaments in the early days of their marriage—and two, she'd asked him last night if this relationship they were floundering through was just sex.

She'd tried to be matter-of-fact, but he knew that she wanted there to be more.

Iris wanted him back, he knew it in his gut. She wanted to pick up where they'd left off thirty years ago, before they'd been torn in two by her illness.

But he couldn't offer that. He couldn't offer her much more, yet. Every time he thought about asking her to stay, he imagined what would happen if she left again.

He imagined the pain which made him remember that long-ago night and the way his life had been gutted and his boys abandoned and destroyed. And between the memory and the imagined pain, he was paralyzed.

But he could play Scrabble. It wasn't much. But it was something.

"Triple word score," Iris bragged, competition always making her feisty. The low light from the table lamp beside them erased some of the lines on her face, cast her skin in gold so she looked luminous. Young. He hoped that it did the same to him.

"That's not how you spell *pigmy,*" he protested, just to get her going.

"Are you challenging?" Her black eyebrow lifted like a delicate wing and he wanted to kiss her so much, his lips hurt.

"No," he said. "But I am calling you a cheater."

"Tough words, Mr. Mitchell," she teased him right back, her eyes glowing. She was so lovely. Every inch of her.

Painfully aware of the bed behind them—their new marriage bed these past few days—he tried to concentrate on the tiles in front of him. Three T's and no vowels.

Always his luck.

She scribbled her score on the pad at her elbow and he rested his hand against hers. He could play Scrabble all night if she wanted him to, but he couldn't do it without touching her. She smiled at him, her shiny silver and black hair against her cheek.

"You're beautiful," he whispered.

"You're trying to distract me because you're losing," she said.

"I always lose this game to you," he said. "Doesn't change how pretty you are."

She stood, crossed the small distance between them to slide herself into his lap, curling her body into his chest the way she always used to.

"I don't want to play games anymore," she whispered, her eyelids heavy, her gaze on his mouth.

"Thank God." He groaned before pulling her as close as he could and swooping in to touch his lips to hers. To find her tongue, the soft damp secrets of her mouth. The smell and taste of her that he never tired of. She arched to him, a tidal wave all down his body.

"Mom?"

Jonah's voice was like a crack in the night. Patrick and Iris jumped. They were startled but couldn't move, as if time had stopped and they were paralyzed. And when Jonah opened the door, poked his head into the cabin, he found them.

Sitting like lovers, their lips damp from kissing.

Jonah blinked at them, his face unmoving, so still it was eerie. Iris jumped off Patrick's lap.

"Jonah," she whispered, her hand out as if he was a deer she was trying to tame. "I'm—" But the expression on his face—part horror, part blame—was a brick wall and she stopped. Her hand fell and she turned her face aside as though she couldn't meet her son's eyes anymore.

Shame ran out of her body like sand from a bag and Patrick nearly gasped, glad he was sitting down, or he'd be on his butt from shock.

How could she feel that way about him? Patrick's stomach rolled at the thought that what was between them had been shameful to Iris. That's why she didn't want Jonah to know. It wasn't about Jonah being hurt, it was about her being ashamed.

Patrick felt dirty, sick that she had felt that way about his touch. That his kisses had made her cheap.

"What are you doing, Mom?" Jonah finally asked.

"I'm trying to be happy," Iris said, lifting her chin, but the look in her eye belied that gesture. And Patrick realized that Iris only felt ashamed in front of Jonah—as if the two of them understood she should know better than to be with Patrick.

Now Patrick was ashamed.

"For how long?" Anger was beginning to make an appearance in Jonah's voice, the red flush of his skin.

Patrick stood. "Jonah—"

"I'm talking to my mom!" Jonah yelled, not bothering at all to hide his rage. "How long, Mom?" he asked, controlling himself slightly while talking to Iris. "Has he made you any promises?"

"This is between your mother and I—" Patrick didn't get to finish because Jonah leaped from the doorway, grabbed Patrick's shoulder and smashed him against the wall.

"You broke her heart!" Jonah yelled right in his face. "You ruined her life and I am supposed to stand by and let you do it again?"

Patrick saw stars and he couldn't breathe for a second.

"Jonah." Iris pulled on Jonah's arms but he only shook Patrick harder.

"She suffered for you, *Dad*." His use of the word was a curse. "We both did. She worked three jobs to keep me in school. Did she tell you that?"

Patrick shook his head. The giant wall he'd built around his regret and his shame and his responsibility started to crumble. And the distance he liked between him and Iris, the distance that kept him safe, shrank.

"My grade school principal wanted to date her," Jonah

said. "He'd come over every Saturday night with flowers and movies for us to watch. Like a family. Like a real family. And she'd send him away and spend the rest of the night crying. This went on for a year. Did she tell you that?"

"No," Patrick whispered. He wondered if Jonah knew there were tears in his own eyes. Jonah's grief was a punch in his gut, a knife that twisted.

"All my award ceremonies and graduations that she went to by herself because you would have nothing to do with us. Those nights by my bed when I was sick or hurt. The hospital trips when we were both so scared, we cried for you. Both of us. We prayed to God that you would somehow know that I was sick and she was scared and we were so broke we didn't know how we were going to pay the bills. We prayed that you would show up. But you never did. All those years we waited for another letter. A change of heart. Something that would let us be a family. And it never came. Did it?"

"Jonah," Patrick breathed, wanting this river of words to stop because he was drowning in everyone's grief. They were all drowning. Tears were seeping down Jonah's cheeks and Patrick, desperate for any connection, any touch, tried to pat Jonah's shoulders. "I didn't know, Jonah. You have to believe me. If I had known, I would have been there. I wish I had been there."

For a second, the briefest moment of hope, Jonah looked on the edge of caving, all the hate and anger and rage in him wavered and Patrick saw the hurt kid in there.

Jonah lowered his head, as if it was too heavy and he rested it against Patrick's chest.

Oh, son. Patrick couldn't breathe through the pain, but he lifted his hands and touched his son's head, stroked his hair.

Jonah pressed his head hard against Patrick, as if he could break through the skin, through the muscle and bones. To the beating heart of his father.

"I'm sorry, son," Patrick whispered.

And Jonah jerked away.

Patrick talked fast, hoping to hold him, to keep that moment. "I'm sorry for what you went through as a kid. I'm sorry I wasn't there to teach you how to stand up for yourself and help—" Jonah looked at his mother, betrayed.

Patrick wished he could suck back every word.

"I don't need your apologies," Jonah finally said, through gritted teeth. "I don't need you. This is about my mother. About what you are doing to her."

Jonah pushed him against the wall once more with re-strained violence, as if he was barely stopping himself from pushing Patrick right through the drywall and logs.

"Did he make you promises, Mom?" Jonah asked Iris, the tender change in him so dramatic that it took a moment for Patrick to register what the boy was saying. And once he did, dread filled him. Patrick was damned by his own cowardice. His own stupidity.

Iris shook her head. "He didn't," she whispered.

"Have you forgotten how hard it was?" Jonah asked. "How much he hurt you? Us?"

"Not for a minute," Iris said, her black eyes bright.

"Then what are you doing?"

Iris's smile was so sad, so resigned. "I don't really know, Jonah. It's just been so nice—" she swallowed "—to pretend."

She touched Jonah's face, stroked the hard planes of his jaw, and the wildness in the boy was tamed. The boy's shoulders slumped and his face relaxed, almost melted into a look like grief. "Happiness isn't free, Jonah," she said. "To be happy you have to sacrifice something."

"He makes you happy?" Jonah asked, as if the very thought was horrific.

Iris nodded, serene and calm, and Patrick felt lifted by something. Some feeling that was too big to name, too strong to see.

"Do you love him?" Jonah asked her, his voice breaking. "After everything he's done?"

Iris glanced at Patrick and he could feel her love, all the love he'd been ignoring since they'd started sleeping together. He leaned back against the wall, suddenly without strength.

Iris didn't say anything, didn't face her son, instead she looked right at Patrick.

I love you, her eyes said. *I love you with all your mistakes. All your pride. Are you brave enough? Are you strong enough for me? Because I love you and I am here.*

"I love you, Mom. But you're a fool," Jonah said and left.

ACID FLOWED through Jonah's veins and he wanted to go back there and smash Patrick's nose in. He wanted to beat the man bloody for even knowing what he seemed to know about Jonah's childhood. But mostly Jonah wanted to kill him for what he was doing to Mom, again.

Jonah should have grabbed her, pulled her out of there and gotten her away from Patrick, back to reality where she'd see that she was only going to be hurt in the end.

Happy? he thought, incredulous. The acid bubbled and his stomach churned. *What does happy have to do with anything?* And how long could it possibly last? Happy wasn't real. Who made decisions based on happiness? Who put themselves at such risk, such personal peril just to be happy for a few minutes?

But she was an adult. Mom knew what she was doing and that somehow made it all worse—that she stood there willingly, ready to take the pain that would no doubt come.

His body shook and he wanted to put his fist through the wall. God, it would be great if Gabe were here. Just showed up out of the blue and Jonah could finally punch something.

He stopped, braced himself against one of the cottages. The rough wood digging into his hand, the cool night air filling his lungs.

Drying his wet face.

Christ, he'd been crying.

He rubbed his face against the cotton of his shirt sleeve. Why had he admitted those things? Good God. He'd told Patrick he used to pray for him to arrive, like some kind of angel in his hospital room?

He barely remembered doing that. Strange that the memory had just been sitting there, waiting.

Jonah rested the top of his head against the building, feeling a terrible weakness, a breathlessness fill him. Reminding him of those nights as a kid when there wasn't enough air in the world for his starving lungs.

Great. Just what I need.

His inhaler was in the Jeep. He tilted his head, trying to get past the moment. Into the next moment. He thought of water.

But his chest got tighter. His breath shorter.

Jonah looked up at the stars and struggled for air. He'd thought he was over it. That he'd buried all of his hurt feelings and foolish hopes for a father in the past, where they belonged.

But he'd seen his mother kissing Patrick and everything had rushed back.

Breath rattled and stalled in his chest. He gasped, his lungs filling with cement. His throat closing.

Water. Air. Daphne.

He thought of Daphne. He thought of those black gloves. Her sweet smile. He thought of the touch of her hands, the weight of her head against his shoulder. He thought of her laugh.

And the moment expanded. He sucked a shallow breath.

He thought of her standing up to him. To her ex-husband on behalf of the kids. He thought of her drinking champagne. Eating oysters one-handed.

He sucked in another breath. And another.

He thought of her on that bed. Asking him to explain his feelings. He thought of how he'd talked to her, made love to her with his eyes wide-open.

Air trickled down his throat, and he took careful sips, until his world opened up past the rattle and kick of his faulty lungs.

Oh, Daphne. Thank you.

Disoriented momentarily by the adrenaline surging through him, it took him a second to locate his car and stumble to it. It took three tries to open the glove box. Finally, he got to his inhaler. Took two puffs and slowly felt the iron bars that lived in his chest relax.

The moon crept out from behind clouds, and suddenly he could see so much clearer. His life, before coming here, stretched out like a familiar road before him.

I don't have any reason to stay here anymore.

He pulled out his cell phone, stared at it as if it was a loaded weapon.

There was no one to protect. Iris was making her own bed to lie in. There was only Daphne and that was never meant to last. They both knew that. Understood that.

He flipped open the phone.

Daphne would be hurt. They both would be. But it would pass, in the end, because—

"We weren't meant to last," he whispered as if saying it out loud made it more official.

Tonight, his mother, Patrick, were proof of that, right? Love didn't last. Happiness was fleeting.

He pressed the phone to his mouth, feeling it against his teeth. Had that gut-wrenching mix of satisfaction and lust and delight he'd experienced with Daphne been happy?

It wasn't anything he'd felt before, but maybe he'd never been happy before.

For a moment in the cabin, with his mother, he'd recognized the look on his mother's face. The light that had shone from her, changing her. Changing the circumstances from something sad and tawdry into something redemptive and clean.

He'd seen that look on Daphne's face when he'd made love to her in the shower, doing unbelievable things to her, pushing both of them past friendly sex into something darker.

Her expression had been angelic. And he'd felt an answering glow on his own face.

Last night, watching Daphne sleep, her mouth open, her face relaxed, he'd felt brighter, sharper. As if he'd taken a drug that made the world more real, somehow. And his place in it more comfortable, as if his life before Daphne had never fit properly, like a suit that was too big.

Jonah wondered, briefly, if he would ever feel that comfort again.

Shaking his head, he amputated the thoughts. Forced them away. Incinerated them.

He and Daphne weren't meant to last. Life went on. Happiness was fleeting. And in the end, they'd had great sex. That's all.

He called Gary. "I'll see you at the office tomorrow. I'm coming back." He disconnected and looked up at the sky through the window of his Jeep. He counted stars until his eyes stopped burning.

Now all he had left to do was pack.

And say goodbye to Daphne.

CHAPTER FOURTEEN

"WELL?" Iris said after Jonah had left and Patrick still could not lift himself from the wall. Without the wall at his back Patrick was pretty sure he'd crumple. "Aren't you going to say anything?"

"Why didn't you tell me?" he finally asked. "About the money and about—" he swallowed "—the principal."

"Because," she said, her chin up. He couldn't look at her directly because her pride burned so bright. So he glanced at her, taking small mental samples, then had to look to the ceiling. The floor. Anywhere but those eyes that were scourging him. "Those were my decisions. Not dating that man, working those jobs instead of asking for help from you were the decisions I made."

Her words, so angry and sad, were like a knife at his throat. He could barely speak.

"And," she continued, "I take responsibility for those decisions." She paused, and he was aware that something was happening here, something he'd been running from. Reckoning had come and she was lethal.

"What about you?" she asked.

"What about me?" he asked, jumping slightly at the tone in her voice. Accusation had crept in and he didn't like it. He'd nearly been beaten by his son tonight, the last thing he needed was to be called to task by a woman who had walked out on him and his boys in the middle of the night. He felt that grudge rebuild the walls around his sense of righteousness.

She left, he thought, gaining strength. *She kept my son a secret.*

"Do you take responsibility for writing those letters?"

"Of course," he said. "And I told you, it was the right thing to do, at the time."

Her lips trembled slightly and she pressed them together. "Okay. I understand that. You wanted to punish me for leaving you but I didn't make you stay celibate. I didn't keep you from moving on. I sent you divorce papers. You didn't sign them."

"I married you in front of God," he said through clenched teeth. He didn't like where this was going. She'd left him. He had nothing to feel guilty about. Dammit. "Papers don't change that."

Tears filled her eyes and Patrick felt his stomach bottom out. He hated to see her cry. Always had. They didn't need to do this, hash out this old business. Not when things were so good right now.

"Baby—" He reached for her and she held up her hand, stopping him.

"Then is this punishment?" she asked. "Are you sleeping with me and hating me at the same time?"

"No." He gasped, feeling her pain like a punch to the gut. "No, honey, no. It's not like that."

"Then what is it like?" she cried. "Why didn't you let me go when you had the divorce papers? Why did you wait for me to come to you again, after all these years? I've slept with you every night and asked for no promises. I've kept this our secret, but I don't know what you're thinking."

"What do you want from me?"

"I want you to take responsibility. So we can move on."

"Move on to what?" he cried. A future? It seemed impossible. It *was* impossible. Jonah made it impossible. The past made it impossible. Patrick's own fears, his constant, nagging, paralyzing fear, made it impossible.

"To whatever's next." She reached out to him, touched his fists, where they were balled at his sides. He felt her skin, her heat in his heart, in his head, down to his feet.

"I love you, Patrick." She smiled as though loving him was something joyful. Yet she stood there nearly crying. "I never stopped. And I know you love me, but you are so angry with me, so tied to the idea that I'm going to leave you again, that you can't let go of the past."

"And taking responsibility for those letters is going to change that?" he asked, incredulous. He'd already done that and they were no closer to a future. They were still in limbo.

"Taking responsibility for your part in the mistakes we *both* made. Yes, I think so."

"You wanted me to divorce you?" How could she talk of love and divorce in the same sentence? It went against everything he felt. Didn't she understand that? Didn't she know that he could only divorce her if he didn't love her anymore?

"I'm saying you should have set me free if you didn't want me. I didn't need a promise to be your lover, Patrick. But if I'm going to stay here now, I am going to need one. And if you can't do that, you have to set me free."

Free? he thought, panicked and angry. *As in, she would leave?*

"What kind of promise?"

"The kind we made on our wedding day. That we'll see each other through the good times and bad, that we will forgive each other the big and small mistakes we make, the hurt we might cause. That we will love each other without rancor or grudge."

She'd reiterated their vows perfectly and he couldn't say anything. His whole body was stone, unfeeling and heavy. Thick.

"Can you do that, Patrick?"

He knew she would walk out if he didn't say something. He opened his mouth but there was only the rattle of his own fear, the gasp and sigh of his cowardice.

Her tears fell, silver streams down her face, unending, like blood from a wound. And still he couldn't say anything.

"I think you better leave," she said, her voice broken. Weak.

"Iris, I can't just—"

"You've had thirty years, Patrick. Please go, I have to pack."

"You're leaving?" he yelled, anger rushing in to strengthen his legs, add fuel to his fire. "Just like that? Oh, I forgot, that's what you do."

Color blanched from her face and her eyelids flinched. "Do you want me to stay so you can keep hurting me like this?" she asked. "Because I can't do it. I won't let you ruin what I feel for you. What we had. You either grow up and deal with your part in this, or leave."

He found the strength to stand, to walk past her without touching her. To do what she wanted, even though he knew it meant she would go.

But despite the agony ripping him apart, he couldn't find the strength to change himself so she would stay.

DAPHNE WOKE up in a rush, her heart thundering in her ears. Sweat trickled down her chest under the old Farmers Do It In The Dirt T-shirt she'd worn to bed.

"It's a raccoon," she whispered to her knotted stomach and empty room. The answering silence was so thick she could actually feel it pressing down on her.

Of course, it was a raccoon. She took a deep breath, almost laughing as her muscles relaxed. What else could it be at— she checked the clock on her bedside table—3:00 a.m.?

She really didn't want to think about what else it could be at 3:00 a.m.

Rattle. Clang.

That raccoon was trying to break in the screen door, she realized and pushed the thin sheet off her body, unwilling to really consider that the raccoon might be something else. Something human.

She grabbed the old Louisville Slugger Helen had left in the hallway—despite being threatened with grounding if she didn't return it to the garage. Now, of course, Daphne was glad that Helen hadn't listened.

She crept down the stairs, hugging the shadows.

Please be a raccoon. Please be a raccoon.

She tightened her sweaty grip on the bat and peered over the top of the gingham curtains.

The raccoon was a man.

She could see a head of brown hair in the shine of the light over the kitchen door.

Oh God, oh God, oh God. She paused, standing on one shaking leg.

She thought of her daughter, her baby, asleep upstairs and

knew she and this bat were the only things between Helen and whatever lunatic was trying to break into their home.

Adrenaline surged through her system.

Before she could second-guess herself, she lunged across the mudroom and whipped open the door, bringing down the baseball bat, one-handed, with all of her might.

Jonah grabbed the bat before it connected with his forehead.

"Jonah," she snapped, her stomach dropping to her feet. "What are you doing here? I almost killed you."

"No, you didn't," he said, his face in the shadows beyond the light. "You swing like a girl."

Heat and joy and a strange foreboding filled her like helium in a balloon. She tugged on her end of the bat, pulling him under the light.

Jonah had been crying. At her gasp he pulled away back to the shadows but she couldn't let him go. She dropped the bat and grabbed his arms.

"What's wrong, Jonah? What happened?"

He shook his head, looking at his feet like a boy caught doing something wrong. Whatever had happened had hurt him terribly. Or was hurting him terribly.

"I know it's late," he said, "but I wanted to see you. I—"

He was here to say goodbye. He didn't have to say anything, she could smell it on him. She nearly doubled over from the pain.

Don't do it! part of her yelled. *You can't bring him into your home, make love to him in your bed and watch dry-eyed when he walks away. You can't do this, Daphne. This will hurt.*

"Jonah." She sighed, torn. But then he dropped the bat and pulled her into his arms as though she was the only thing that could save him.

His breath shuddered in his chest. His hands fisted her hair.

She could feel the steady, heavy beat of his heart against hers. And she knew whether she let him in right now or sent him away, she wouldn't be dry-eyed.

It already hurt, how could it hurt worse? The damage was done.

And her decision was made. She pulled him into her home, the one she bought herself and shared with her daughter. She led him up the stairs to her bedroom, with its flowered cotton sheets and sensible cotton underwear in the dresser.

She laid him down in her bed. Without the gloves or the champagne. With just her heart bursting with love for him, she pulled off his shirt and kissed his chest. Pressed her hands to his heart.

Goodbye, her body sighed.

"Do you regret…this?" he whispered, as if they were in a church. "I mean, do you wish we hadn't made love?" And she knew what he was asking, it was there in his eyes, the sad set to his lips. *Are you happy even though I'm going to leave?* he was asking. *Are you happy despite knowing that unhappiness is coming?*

"No," she whispered. "I'm glad."

He groaned and sat up, pulling her across his lap, so she straddled him. She could tell something was running loose in him and all the careful seduction of the night in New York was gone, the measured roughness, the erotic game-playing eroded under whatever demons were riding him.

It was just him, Jonah, vulnerable and naked.

And it was just her, Daphne, vulnerable and stupid.

But she was okay with that if it gave her one more night with him.

She opened the fly to his pants and found him with her hand. He was already hard, hot, his blood beating just as heavy in his erection as it was in his chest.

He groaned at her touch, his hands sliding under her shirt to find her waist, her breasts.

"I don't have a condom," she said, almost willing to risk it. Almost hoping she might get pregnant.

Her entire body contracted hard at the thought. Longing rippled down her spine. A baby. Another baby. How wonderful would that be?

But Jonah was digging into his back pocket, pulling his pants down to his knees as he retrieved the condom.

Better this way, she thought, taking it from his hands. Better to be safe. But part of her wanted that baby. That chance. Who knew when it would come again? Prince Charmings weren't just lying around her pumpkin patch waiting for her.

Lifting herself, she sheathed him in the condom then slid down, stopping halfway, the sensations almost too much. Loving him almost seemed to hurt. Panicked, she gasped, shaking and clutching at his shoulders. Not sure if she was pushing him or pulling him, afraid of what she felt and afraid of never feeling it again.

It was as though he was already gone, and the pain was stunning.

How can I do this to myself?

"I'm here," he whispered. "I'm right here, Daphne."

The strength of him grounded her. His arms at her waist supported her. His blue eyes glowed in the moonlight, holding her as surely as his hands did, as carefully as her body held his.

"Take me," he groaned.

Her muscles relaxed, the pain eased and it was only bone-deep pleasure. She sank all the way down, taking him in so deep, so hard she knew even when he was gone, she'd feel him there.

Probably for the rest of her life.

DAPHNE'S SKIN was silver in the faint light, the fine muscles of her back stood out in erotic relief. She was so beautiful. And he'd never expected this to hurt so much. He'd never expected to be so damn sad.

He stroked her spine and rolled so he could see her profile. He was surprised by the stream of tears that rolled down her face. The sobs that began to rack her naked body.

"Oh, Daph—"

"Go," she whispered. "Just…leave. Don't say anything."

Not wanting to hurt her more, he did as she asked. He pulled on his pants, his shirt. Shoved his bare feet into his shoes because he knew the longer he stayed in this room with her the worse it would be.

He crept down the hall past Helen's room and wanted, stupidly, to say goodbye to the girl. But that was the last thing Daphne wanted, so like some kind of thief he skulked down the stairs and slipped out the back door, feeling with every step, every beat of his heart as though he was leaving some unknown part of himself behind.

The new part. The laughter and the fun that the Larson girls had mined out of him. That fleeting sense of happiness. Of rightness. Those weren't going with him back to the city.

But he couldn't stay. Not so close to the Mitchells and not after what he'd done to Daphne tonight. His life wasn't here.

He started the Jeep, his duffel bag in the back, and drove toward the highway and the city. Away from Daphne.

The highway was practically empty and he headed south. Caught the Jersey turnpike toward New Brunswick and was home in record time. He parked in the underground lot and waved at the security guard.

He lived on the top floor of his first condo development. Riding up the steel and glass elevator that ran up the side of the building usually stroked his ego. The view was incredible. Everything as it should be.

But this time it was hollow. Empty. The Manhattan skyline was too jagged. Too sharp. It didn't have the rounded big muscles of the Catskill Mountains and the Hudson River was different down here. Foreign.

He stepped into his condo, dropped the duffel on the marble tiles, and for the first time, realized how quiet his condo was. How utterly still.

It's like a tomb, he thought, and a chill ran up his spine.

Glancing into his kitchen, outfitted with all the top-of-the-line appliances he didn't use, he knew there was no food for him to eat. His freezer utterly devoid of Popsicles.

His walls were covered in black and white photographs that someone else took, of places he'd never been, of people he didn't know.

There were no scrapbooks, no pictures on his fridge, no clutter, no mess. No nothing.

This was his home and it looked as though no one lived in it. Certainly not him.

God, what am I doing? A panic so profound, like running headfirst into a brick wall, tightened his throat. Luckily his inhaler was in his pocket and he took two quick puffs before the attack got worse.

He left Daphne behind for this? For an empty home and work that he could do from anywhere?

He stepped to the floor-to-ceiling window, staring at the skyline that used to excite him. Challenge him. He felt nothing. They were just buildings.

Is this what I want? It had been so long since he'd thought about what he wanted that he wasn't even sure he knew.

He used to want to make money so his mother would be taken care of. Then he'd wanted to do a little bit of good for the planet. Then he'd thought of Haven House. But even Haven House seemed like a burden at the moment.

Everything was a chore. Something to get through. And suddenly his life stretched out in front of him. Every day something to survive, an ordeal to endure.

"I'm never going to jump in an inflatable castle again," he said aloud. *I'm never going to see Daphne again, much less have sex with her.*

That thought had him reaching for his inhaler.

How was it possible that it took more courage to choose to be happy? To swallow his pride and fix what was wrong in his family so he could be with Daphne, than to live the sort of mundane soulless existence he'd been living? His life was a prison and he'd stupidly just incarcerated himself again.

Jonah would have done anything for his mother, except forgive his father. It dawned on him, that in order to have Daphne, he was going to have to do the unthinkable.

Let go of all his anger at his father.

Otherwise, how was he ever going to live?

What was his life without Daphne?

Giant, immovable objects that had been crowding his chest since he was a boy, shifted. Anger and hate and resentment were pushed aside by a courage he didn't know he possessed. And suddenly, where he didn't think there was room, there was a vast cavern and Daphne just moved right into his heart.

He saw his father more clearly—his motivations, confused and compounded by love and desperation, had forced him into mistakes he clearly wished he could take back.

The man wanted to do the right thing and Jonah, in order to have Daphne in his life, would let him.

He rested his head against the wall and stared at a black and white photo of a sailboat under full sail.

Jonah had never been on a sailboat.

"Oh my God," he muttered, pushing himself into action. "This is ridiculous. I love her and I left her."

He grabbed his duffel bag, his keys and walked out the door.

He'd be back at Daphne's by sunrise.

"MOMMY?" At her daughter's voice Daphne's eyes snapped open. There Helen was, wearing her pink and purple pajamas, her messy hair haloed by the early morning sun. That was normal.

Daphne was in her bed. Normal.

Birds sang outside. Normal.

But her heart lay in pieces in her chest. Her body so cold she'd pulled on two sweatshirts during the long night, and she still wasn't warm.

"Hi, Helen," Daphne said. Longing for her daughter hit her in the sternum and she lifted the covers so Helen could scramble into bed with her. Helen curled into her like a kitten against her belly and Daphne sighed. She would survive this. She had her daughter, her work, her mother, good friends. What did she need love for? The body went on without a working heart—she was proof of that. "What's going on?"

"Was Jonah here last night?"

Daphne stroked her daughter's hair. "Yes, honey, he was."

"But he left?"

For a second she couldn't speak. She couldn't even breathe. But then her daughter's little hand patted her face, wiping away the tears Daphne had been leaking most of the night. "I'm sorry, Mom. I really liked him."

"So did I." Daphne sighed through the pain.

They lay there quietly and Daphne again thanked the powers that be for sending her this little girl. This miracle with blond hair and sticky fingers.

"There's a man at the For Sale sign next door. He's putting a Sold sign on it," Helen said after a while.

Daphne sat up. "Is it Sven?"

Helen shook her head. "Nope. It's a man and a woman. The woman was throwing up. Can we have pancakes for breakfast?"

"Sure thing, honey." With her foot, Daphne dug at the bottom of the bed, finding her underwear. Maybe she could talk to the new owners, find out about buying just half an acre of the land. "See if you can find the mix and I'll be back in a few seconds."

Helen leaped off the bed and beat feet for the kitchen and Daphne shoved her feet into flip-flops. At the very least she'd find out what kind of person spent far too much money for land like that and whether or not they'd be good neighbors.

Of course, the added benefit of their arrival was forcing her to get out of bed, where she could have stayed for the next ten years. Nursing her broken heart.

She took the shortcut through the trees and ran out onto the road right beside a red convertible, surprising the hell out of two people leaning against it.

"Hi," the man said, looking at her then at the tree line

she'd escaped from. He sort of resembled what Einstein must have looked like when he was younger. Rumpled clothes. Hair on end, small glasses in front of incredibly shrewd eyes.

"Hi," she said, catching her breath. "I'm Daphne Larson. I own the farm next door to this land."

"Oh, great," the man said, pushing away from the car. They shook hands and she had to admit he had a good shake. "My name is Gary. My business partner and I just bought this land."

Strange that he referred to the woman beside him, who looked decidedly green around the gills, as a business partner. But maybe that's what young Einsteins did.

"Nice to meet you," Daphne said, holding her hand out to the woman.

"Oh," she said, smiling. Sort of. "I'm not his business partner, I'm Gary's wife, Carrie." Carrie pushed off the car but the motion must have set something off inside of her and she detoured sideways to throw up at the back bumper.

Gary rushed to hold her hair back and pat limply at her waist. "Sorry," he said, wincing as Carrie heaved some more. "My wife is pregnant."

"Oh my gosh," Daphne said, her heart going out to the poor woman. "Please come to my house. I've got Popsicles."

Carrie straightened, wiping her mouth. "That actually sounds edible," she said. Gary looked delighted and surprised as though Popsicles were the answer to a riddle he'd been struggling to figure out.

Gary curled an arm around Carrie's back and took a step then stopped. His gaze was fixed on something over Daphne's shoulder.

"What are you doing here?" he asked. "I thought you were leaving last night."

Daphne turned and saw Jonah, his hands in his pockets, standing in the middle of the road.

His eyes, sad and resigned, were locked on her face.

Her heart surged against her ribs.

Oh God, he came back. That thought ran so loud in her head she couldn't think about anything else.

It was stupid. More stupid than having sex with him in her bed last night. More stupid than falling in love with him in the first place, but she could not control the ecstatic pounding of her heart.

He was staying.

But something wasn't right. How did Gary know Jonah?

Her heart was getting this moment all wrong.

Static filled her head and she embraced it. She held on to it for as long as she could so that she couldn't do the simple math that was staring her in the face. If she stayed stunned like this, she couldn't connect the dots and she wouldn't be the biggest fool in the entire world. She'd just be a woman confused about what her lover, who screwed her and left her last night, had to do with the land he knew she wanted.

"I'm sorry, Ms. Larson, this is my business partner, Jonah Closky," Gary said.

Daphne closed her eyes, a giant chasm opening up under her heart.

CHAPTER FIFTEEN

JONAH JUMPED IN FAST. He knew he had a lot of explaining to do. But he also knew Daphne would understand. After the explaining. Because right now—face pale, eyes closed, hands curled into fists—she didn't look so understanding.

"Daphne." Jonah reached out to her but she flinched away from him. "Listen to me. I did not know we bought that land. I didn't know that night of the gala and I didn't know last night. I swear to you."

He waited. He waited a million little deaths and she didn't say anything. Growing frantic, he turned on Gary.

"You said we didn't buy that land."

"When?" Gary asked.

"Yesterday, on the phone, you said, *no land,*" Jonah said.

"I said, *no land should cost that much.* We had a bad connection," Gary clarified.

Bad connection. Great. His life was falling apart thanks to a bad connection. But he didn't go through what he went through last night, only to give up this morning. He'd driven to the city and back for this woman. He reorganized his life, changed this viewpoint. Decided to find out what happy meant to him. It meant her.

"Daphne, I swear. I didn't know. I didn't even know you were interested in the land until our drive into the city. As soon as we got to the hotel I called Gary and told him not to buy the land." He shot Gary a disgusted look. "Which he didn't do."

"The week before, you said buy the land, so I bought the land," Gary said, throwing his hands up. "Is this some kind of contract dispute, because Sven didn't mention other offers."

"Why would he?" Daphne finally asked, her voice a rasp. "When you offered so much."

What does that mean? Jonah searched her face for clues to what she was thinking, but he got nothing from her.

"It's just money," he said, feeling as though he needed to fill the silence. Her back went straight, her jaw tight and he realized that might not have been the right thing to say. "Look, Daphne, we can give you some of the land."

"Give?" Gary cried. "Have you lost your mind?"

Finally Daphne faced Jonah, her green eyes, through which he could usually read her like a book, were opaque. She'd closed a door on him.

"What are you going to do to the land?" she asked. "Condos?"

He opened his mouth but Gary beat him to it.

"A hotel," Gary said, sealing Jonah's coffin. "A great one. A waterslide and spa. I can show you some drawing—" He finally stopped talking as if cluing in that he'd said something wrong.

Daphne had gone red.

"You were going to put the Mitchells out of business?"

"That was my plan originally," Jonah admitted. "But it's changed."

"It has?" Gary asked.

"I don't care," she said. "You lied."

"I didn't. I—" She glared at him. "All right, I lied by omission. But the point is, we're not going to build a hotel here. We're going to build Haven House here."

"Are you out of your mind?" Gary cried. "We can't take a loss on this land. We just paid a fortune for it."

"I don't care, Gary!" he yelled, feeling everything falling out of his hands. "We're not building a hotel here."

He turned back to Daphne, tried to touch her, hold her, but she slapped his hands away and stepped back.

Daphne shook her head, anger making her face rigid. He was losing her.

"Daphne, I left you last night and I went back to the city and I realized what a mistake I had made walking away from you. My life is totally empty without you."

"Stop, Jonah—"

"No, I won't stop. I can't. I'm ready to go down to the Riverview and forgive my father. I'm ready to give them my blessing to try again, if it means I can live here with you. Make a family with you—"

"Are you nuts?" she cried. "Two weeks ago you meant to drive them out of business."

"That was two weeks ago," he said. "I know it's crazy. I know it makes no sense. But I'm trying to start over, here. I'm trying to be a better man."

"Why?" She shook her head as though she thought it was an impossible goal. "There's no money in it."

That stung. Oh, that really stung. "I love you, Daphne, and I'm not going to walk away."

"You already did."

"And it's a mistake I'm not going to make again."

Gary and Carrie were watching with dropped jaws, eyes

wide and he tried to wave them away, but they ignored him, clearly not wanting to leave their front-row seats.

The longer Daphne was silent the more frantic he felt. So frantic that the last of his unbreakable rules simply crumbled. "I'm begging you, Daphne," he whispered, the words so hard to say. "I'm begging you to give me a chance."

She blinked, her face pale, beautiful. "So you can change your mind in another two weeks?" she asked. "No. I'd be an idiot to believe you, and I've already learned that lesson."

She turned to Gary. "If you try to build a hotel here, the entire community will fight you. You'll have more enemies than you'll know what to do with."

Then, to Jonah's utter despair, she turned and walked away, without even once looking back at him. As if he meant nothing to her.

The stillness she left behind was oppressive. Deafening. Like a giant black hole in the universe.

"So," Gary said, clapping his hand on Jonah's back. "Let me get this straight. You, Jonah Closky, are in love with an organic farmer?"

"I am." He sighed, feeling the weight of every hour he'd been awake. Every moment of his life a knife in his chest. He scrubbed at his eyes. "What am I going to do?"

"What you always do," Gary said, smiling sympathetically. "Win her over."

"How?" he asked. "Maybe you didn't just see her walk away like I'm nothing to her."

"Oh, Jonah," Carrie said, pulling Jonah into a hug that smelled slightly of vomit but he was too heartsick to protest. "She walked away because you mean everything to her. But you've got some serious groveling to do."

"I can grovel," he said. But he wasn't all that convinced

it would work on Daphne. He'd hurt her. Bad. And she wasn't the type to hand out second chances.

He sighed, digging his keys out of his pocket. "Let me further blow your mind and invite you back to the Riverview Inn to introduce you to my family."

"Your what?" Gary asked.

Jonah smiled, wearily. "That's what I used to think. Follow me."

He walked back to Daphne's farm where he'd parked his Jeep, only to find Helen sitting in the driver's seat, wearing a pair of pajamas under a denim jacket.

"You trying to steal my Jeep?" he joked, his heart slightly lighter for seeing the girl.

"No." Helen shook her head then nailed him right in the chest. "You hurt my mom."

"I know," he whispered. "But I'm going to try to make it better."

"Good." She toyed with a button on her jacket. "She loves you."

"You think?"

Helen nodded. "But she thinks you'll leave us. She thinks that about everyone."

"I'm not going anywhere," he said, making it a solemn promise to the girl.

"You better not," she said and stood, poised on the edge of the door frame ready to jump. A little purple and pink daredevil. "Because I like you, too."

And then she jumped right into his arms.

HE DROVE UP to the Riverview only to find Patrick leaning against Iris's car. A Thermos and a stack of sandwiches sat beside him on the trunk.

Gabe and Max sat in lawn chairs with cups of coffee, as if taking in a fireworks show. Max waved as Jonah jumped out of his Jeep wondering what sort of situation he'd stumbled across here.

Jonah directed Carrie and Gary toward his cottage and told them to make themselves comfortable. They left gratefully, probably as tired of all the sudden drama in Jonah's life as he was.

"What's going on here?" Jonah asked, coming up to stand behind his brothers.

His brothers.

He nearly laughed at how ludicrous it all was. It wasn't even 7:00 a.m. and he'd declared his love, had his love rejected, claimed his brothers—at least in his own mind— and was about to bridge the gap with his father all so he and his mother could get on with their lives.

I think I need a drink.

"Well," Gabe said, craning his neck to look at Jonah. "When you stormed out of here last night—"

"Without saying goodbye," Max said, taking a sip of coffee. "Delia and Alice are pissed at you."

"I'm back," Jonah said and something in his tone made both men turn to look at him. He met their gazes and even, after a moment, managed to smile.

Hi, guys, he wanted to say. *I missed you.*

"Are we going to have to have some kind of group hug thing?" Max asked, turning back to his coffee. "Or can we just say we did?"

"I think we can skip the hug," Jonah said, staring at the horizon because his eyes were suspiciously damp.

"Glad to hear it," Gabe said after a moment, his own lips

curled into a slight smile. "I got group-hugged out when Max decided to rejoin the living a while back."

"Bite me, Gabe," Max grumbled, and Jonah smiled. Having brothers was great. Gary hated it when Jonah tried to insult him. "I seem to remember someone getting more than a little weepy and clingy a few months ago when Stella was born."

"Oh, right." Gabe laughed. "Because you were so dry-eyed."

"Look," Jonah interrupted, "as much as I love hearing what pansies you are, maybe it's time someone told me what's going on?"

Gabe and Max exchanged a look that he couldn't quite decipher, probably since he hadn't yet gotten his brother decoder ring.

"Maybe you can talk some sense into our parents," Gabe said.

"Why?"

"Well, Mom is trying to leave," Max said. Jonah didn't even flinch when he said *Mom*. None of them did. He could share his beloved mother, if they were ready to treat her right. And it seemed they were.

"And Dad is sitting on her car, so she won't go," Gabe said. "Now she's holed up in the kitchen. She comes out every five minutes and yells at him, but he just sits there and says he's not moving."

"Is it working?" Jonah asked.

"Well—" Max shrugged "—she hasn't left, but she's getting pretty upset."

Jonah sighed and stepped through the narrow space between the lawn chairs. He hadn't even had coffee yet, for crying out loud. He was running on adrenaline and love.

"Jonah," Patrick said with a curt nod when he approached. "Thought you left last night."

"I didn't get very far," Jonah said, settling down next to the old man. After a minute Patrick offered him a sandwich and Jonah gratefully accepted.

"So, what's your plan?" Jonah asked. "I mean, I get that she can't leave with you on her car. But you can't sit here forever."

"I'm gonna sit here until she sees reason," Patrick said, definitively.

"Yeah?" Jonah took a bite of ham sandwich. "And what's reasonable between you two right now?"

Patrick looked at him, watched him, trying to see down to Jonah's studs and empty spaces. So, Jonah met his stare and let him.

"I don't know," Patrick answered honestly. Jonah had to give him credit for that, considering that last night Jonah had been about to break his nose for looking at Iris wrong. "But I know I can't let her leave."

"What's different from last night?" Jonah asked. "Because last night it didn't seem like you cared much."

"I love your mother," Patrick said. "I'm just a proud, stubborn man and I was an idiot last night. I've been an idiot all week. The second she came back into my life I should have thanked God and done whatever she wanted me to do." Patrick tore off a crust of bread, tossed it onto the gravel at his feet. "I don't know if you can believe that," he said. "I don't know if you can forgive me—"

"I'll give you my blessing," Jonah said and saw Patrick's chin tremble. "I'll tell her to come out here and talk to you, to listen to you. But I need a promise." He beat back the years of anger, the righteous rage, the voices that screamed this man wasn't trustworthy.

"Anything, son." Patrick's voice was a rasp, torn from his gut.

"You can't hurt her again." A swell of emotion made Jonah's skin prickle, his throat thick.

"I won't."

"Promise me," he said. He set down the sandwich and met the moment head-on, emotion and everything. He looked right at his father. "Promise me. Promise me you forgive her. That you'll care for her. That you will reward this risk she's taking by treating her like a queen."

Patrick stood, held out his hand and Jonah took it. Gripped it hard.

"I promise," Patrick said and when Jonah didn't move, didn't turn away, Patrick pulled on Jonah's hand and brought him close. Jonah knew what the old man wanted. What he was going to do if Jonah didn't stop it. But he didn't step away. He let his father pull him closer. Until finally, Patrick's arms were around him, holding him so hard Jonah couldn't move.

Jonah's ribs cracked and tears sat in the corners of his eyes, fat and hot.

"I love you, son," Patrick whispered and Jonah shut his eyes. He knew what he should say. If this were a movie, he'd be able to say it. But it wasn't a movie and the words just weren't ready.

"I can't—"

"I know, son," Patrick said, understanding what Jonah barely could. "It will take some time. But we've got lots of it. Right?"

Patrick pulled back, looking for an answer, and Jonah nodded. "I'm not going anywhere," he said.

"Good." Patrick pounded on Jonah's back.

"I thought we weren't hugging," Max said, just over Jonah's shoulder.

"I'm not hugging you two," Jonah said, taking in these three men who were his family. Were the family he'd dreamed about, and told strangers he had. Big men, honorable. Standing side by side no matter what.

Pieces of his life he'd spent so long pretending he wasn't missing just fell into place.

"Jonah?" His mother's voice at the kitchen door had them all turning.

Iris stepped toward them, her black eyes flashing. "I thought you left," she said.

He smiled slightly to let her know that things were okay. Well, as okay as they could be at the moment. "I'm in love," he said and everyone gasped. *For crying out loud, is it so hard to believe?* "With Daphne."

Mom blinked, fought a smile but not successfully. "Does she love you?"

"She does," he said and winced. "But I don't think she's real happy about it right now."

"What are you going to do?" Iris asked, her gaze ricocheting off Patrick, bouncing to Jonah, then back to Patrick as if he was a magnet. And Patrick stood beside Jonah, practically vibrating at the sight of her.

Love was making fools of all of them.

"I'm going to stick around until she gets happy about it," Jonah answered. "Look, Mom, you were right all along. It takes sacrifices to be happy and being in love is hard and complicated and messy and sometimes requires more of us than we're ready to give."

Her face shut down and she sucked her upper lip between her teeth. He stepped toward her, wrapped her in his arms because he didn't want her to have to fight what she wanted. "It's okay," he told her. "It's okay to love Patrick."

"Oh." She stepped back, looking at Patrick over Jonah's shoulder, her eyes flinging daggers at the man. "I'm fine with it. I've loved that man since the moment I saw him. He's the one with the problem."

They all swiveled to look at Patrick.

"I'm sorry," Patrick said, riveted to Iris. "I'm sorry for the letters. For the silence. But I'm not sorry I didn't divorce you. I'm not sorry for what we've had here the last week."

Iris's breath hiccupped.

"I'm sorry I was so weak last night," Patrick said. "That I made you think I was going to let you walk away from me again. Because I can't." He shook his head. "I won't. You are mine, Iris Mitchell. In front of God, in front of our boys, you are mine."

Well, Jonah thought, *that was pretty good.* He caught Gabe and Max nodding their heads in agreement.

"Mom?" Jonah said when Iris didn't fling herself into Patrick's waiting arms.

"I forgive you," she said to Patrick. Then she waited. She tilted her head and waited longer. They all waited.

"Thank you," Patrick said, tears running down his face. "I forgive you, too."

And with that, Iris went running. Patrick caught her, holding her head so he could kiss her face. He whispered words Jonah couldn't hear into her smiling mouth.

A weight was pulled from Jonah's chest. Guilt and

sorrow that had dogged him and his mother for thirty years just evaporated as if it had never been there. Mom was happy and it was all Jonah had ever wanted.

Now, he thought, wondering if it was too early to start drinking, *if only Daphne could be so easily persuaded.*

"Nice job, Jonah," Gabe said. He and Max had the folding chairs under their arms.

Max nodded in agreement, but his obsidian eyes weren't quite warm. "What's the story with Daphne?"

Jonah groaned and looked heavenward. "I need a drink."

"Ah," Gabe's arm landed across Jonah's shoulder and the two men steered him inside. "I remember that feeling."

"Me, too," Max said with a smile. "I'll get the scotch."

CHAPTER SIXTEEN

JONAH STAYED.

It had been two and a half weeks since she'd told him to go and he wasn't budging.

Daphne stared out the window over the sink at the land across the fence from her pumpkin patch. There were trucks on that land, taking away the rubble from the buildings that were being torn down. Crews had come and gone, surveying the property. Guys in hard hats stayed for a day, rolling out blueprints, then, after nodding their heads and slapping each other on the back, they all left.

But not Jonah.

Daphne hired another delivery guy so she never went to the Riverview. And Jonah had, in turn, hired her delivery guy and the truck to take the food down to the school. Which was fine with her. She was happy to help. Happier that she didn't have to sit in that truck cab with Jonah every day.

But every day he came up to the land.

Helen, the little spy, told Daphne that Jonah spent all day knocking down the old buildings himself. With a sledgehammer. So that the land would be ready for the residences he had planned, and the classrooms and basketball court he wanted for Haven House. Helen claimed he packed a lunch and at the end of the day Patrick, Gabe or Max would stop by to bring him a beer.

Every night he went back to the Riverview but every morning he returned.

With gifts.

The first morning it had been the newspaper and a cup of hot coffee sitting on the front stoop. Like a child, he'd rung the doorbell and left before she got there.

Then it had been oysters packed in dry ice. And sushi from New York delivered at dinnertime.

Then the flowers started. Black-eyed Susans and clover from the roadside tucked into the beer bottles. Yesterday tulips were delivered from the city. The day before, a rosebush had been planted by her back door.

Day by day, minute by minute, he was wearing her down, chipping away at all her anger and doubt. Mining under her righteous reasons for walling him out.

He'd obviously made up with his family. He'd kept his promise about Haven House.

"Hey, Mom," Helen cried, the front door slamming in its casing behind her.

"How many times do I have to tell you not to slam the door?" Daphne grumbled, so stressed and strung out about Jonah she was getting snippy with Helen, who didn't deserve it.

"Lots," Helen said, unfazed by snippy Mommy. "Look what came for you."

Daphne cranked off the water and wiped her hands on a tea towel, dying to see what Jonah had in store for her, yet, at the same time, not wanting to see. *I'm not strong enough for this,* she thought. *I'm too weak and I'll let him in and he'll go. He'll leave and it will hurt so much because I love him more than I've loved any man.*

But of course, she looked at the long, thin box wrapped in a purple bow, with a small card tucked under the ribbon, that Helen held. And her heart sang.

"Where'd you find it?" Daphne asked.

"On the front step. You gonna open it?"

No. She should just get rid of the box, without opening it. Perhaps take it over to him and demand he stop with these childish games so they could both move on with their lives.

"Oh, Mom." Helen sighed as though Daphne was the biggest disappointment. "I'll do it. You open the card." Helen thrust the tiny card at Daphne and went to work on the ribbon.

With trembling hands Daphne opened the envelope.

I miss you, it read, in thick masculine handwriting. *I miss us.*

"Oh, cool," Helen cooed, lifting out a pair of long black silk gloves.

"Oh my Lord," Daphne cried, grabbing the gloves out of Helen's hands like they were dynamite. The gloves— No, they weren't *the* gloves. They were new gloves.

She groaned and dropped her head into the balled-up silk in her hand.

"Mom," Helen said after a moment, her little hands patting at her shoulders. "Do you like Jonah?"

Daphne sighed heavily. *Like* him, as if they were fifth-graders? That didn't even begin to cover it.

"Yes," she said, "but it's complicated."

"Complicated like it is with Daddy?" Helen asked and Daphne lifted her head.

"No," she said. "Not like that. Complicated in a different way."

"Daddy asked out Josie's teacher. They're going on dates."

Daphne dropped her head back into the gloves. Ah, just the sort of cheery pick-me-up she needed to hear. "Good for Daddy," she mumbled.

"Do you love Jonah?"

Daphne reached out to stroke the end of her daughter's braid. Helen's hair was turning more blond with the increasing summer sun. The strands seemed almost white like when she was a baby. Changing.

Me, too, she thought. *I'm changing. I can't stop this. I am powerless.*

"Yes," Daphne finally answered. "I love Jonah."

"He loves you, too," Helen said.

"How do you know?" Daphne smiled, laughing slightly at her daughter's hubris.

"He told me."

"When?" The traitor. She was supposed to be spying for Daphne!

"I have a life, Mom," Helen said, rolling her eyes. "I go over there sometimes and we talk."

"What do you talk about?" Daphne asked, almost afraid to. Something big and thick was rolling through her, starting in her stomach and building through her chest. Like steam in a kettle, it kept building and building and she didn't know how long she could keep it in.

Helen shrugged. "About what he's building. And what it will be like there for the kids and moms from the city. And we talk about school and boys and Jerry the Gerbil—"

Just like that Daphne blew. She stalked out of the house.

"I like him, Mom," Helen cried, coming after her. "You shouldn't worry about him leaving."

"Why's that?" Daphne asked, turning around, angry

and upset by the gloves and the flowers and the conversations he was having with Helen.

"Because," Helen said, "he's not going anywhere. Mom, if you love him and he loves you, why don't you just be together? Why are you making this so hard?"

"Because he screwed up!" Daphne yelled. "He made mistakes."

"So?" Helen asked, shrugging. "I keep slamming the door, but you forgive me."

It was hardly the same thing. Right?

So she spun on her heel and followed the sounds of deconstruction happening on the adjoining land. She stomped through her pumpkin patch and climbed over the old fence only to come face to sweaty back with Jonah.

Going to work on what was left of the old barn, he wore gloves and a sweat-stained red shirt that clung to him. His whole body flexed and shifted as he swung the sledgehammer into the rotting oak, tearing it down bit by bit, as if he'd been doing manual labor all his life.

Daphne's throat was a sand trap and all her anger coalesced into something hotter. Something more dangerous.

Oh, her body cried, those unruly hormones starting a ruckus, *we want that one!*

"Hey, Jonah!" Helen said with a big wave.

He stopped and pulled his sunglasses off. The smile that lit his face at the sight of them hit Daphne right at the knees and her whole body went wobbly.

"Hi, girls," he said, wiping his forehead with his arm and Daphne thought maybe she should shield Helen's eyes from something that, to Daphne, was so X-rated it shouldn't be viewed in broad daylight.

"I see you got my gift," Jonah said after a moment. She

just stared at him, still reeling from the potent sexual appeal of him. "The gloves," he clarified.

Right. The gloves she was so mad about. "What are you doing?"

"Well—" he took a big breath and looked at the skeleton frame of the barn "—I'm tearing this down so I can build a cafeteria and—"

"With me," she said, lifting the gloves clenched in her fist. "With these."

"I'm giving them to you," he said slowly, as though she might not understand his language and Helen, behind her, giggled. "Because I like you."

"Well, stop," Daphne said.

He shook his head.

"What?"

"I am not going to stop."

"To what end, Jonah? What do you want?"

His smile was so sweet, so sure, his beloved face lit with something she could only call happiness. "I want you to marry me," he said.

She nearly stumbled backward. *Marry?* He'd never said anything about marriage. About vows. About permanence. Her head spun.

"Yes!" Helen pumped her fist. "We're getting married."

"Helen." Daphne sighed. "Could you go back to the house? I need to talk to Jonah alone for a second."

Helen looked mutinous but finally she agreed. "I'm going, Mom, but my vote is we keep him," she said, pointing to Jonah before turning tail and leaving.

"I've got your kid's vote," Jonah quipped. "What do I have to do to win yours?"

"When are you leaving?"

"Daphne, I'm staying."

"For how long?"

He blinked. "For as long as you'll have me."

Oh God, it was so what she wanted to hear. So what she wanted to believe.

"Have you told your family about your plan to put them out of business?"

He nodded. "I told them a few nights ago."

"And?"

"And, Gabe laughed." Jonah shrugged. "He said he would have done the same thing if he'd been in my shoes."

Daphne gasped. How could they forgive him so easily?

"Don't use the land thing as an excuse, Daphne. It's water under the bridge."

His eyes bored into hers with an intensity that made her light-headed. She was dizzy with her feelings for him. Anger and hurt mixed with desire and love. How was she supposed to make sense of this?

"Daphne—" He reached for her and she flinched away, feeling too raw to be touched by him. Too unstable to trust herself.

"No more gifts. Please. Don't talk to my daughter. Don't try to see me." She turned away, needing terribly to get away from him. But he grabbed her hand, pulled on her when she tried to yank herself free.

"I'm staying, not just for Haven House, but for you," he whispered and when he wouldn't let go of her she shut her eyes. Blocked him out. "I sold my condo. Moved in with my family. I'm watching my parents kiss all damn day. I realized after we made love and I left that my life is empty without you. I'm not going to walk away from you without a fight. This is my life now. My family. Haven House and you."

She shook her head.

"You don't believe me?" he asked and she knew he was wounded but she forced herself not to care. Better now, better these minor hurts and pains rather than what would happen later, after Helen was attached and Daphne was deeper in love.

"I think you mean it now," she said. "But you could change your mind. Are you going to mean it three weeks from now? How about during the winter, or five years from now? Or six? Or when Helen—"

"I'm not Jake," he said, his eyebrows snapping together in irritation. "And I am not your father. I am not going to leave you."

"You don't know that," she cried. "You said it yourself, there are no guarantees."

"I am," he said fiercely. He pressed her hands to his heart. "I am a sure thing. And you love me."

She turned her head away. She couldn't keep her feelings hidden. But it hurt that she was so transparent to him when she couldn't read him at all.

"You do. You love me," he insisted. "And I..." He took a big breath. "I love you."

That was enough. She jerked her hands away and shoved him back a step. "Please," she snapped. "You barely understand the concept."

"You're right!" He laughed, flinging his arms out. "I'm a total idiot when it comes to this stuff. I'm screwed up about my parents and my brothers—but I'm trying. I have no clue what happy is, except that it's what you make me feel. So, you're right. I barely understand what it means to be happy or in love. I'm just figuring it out, because of you."

"That hardly sounds like a guarantee," she said. "It sounds like a disaster."

"I know. But I think that's what love is."

She shook her head, unable to be convinced. Sick to her stomach, right now love was the worst thing that had happened to her.

His eyes sparked with sudden anger and he dropped the hammer, grabbing her in his arms. His touch gentle but hard, and memories of New York flooded her. "I'm not going anywhere," he said through clenched teeth. His breath, coffee-scented and hot, brushed her face and her body couldn't stop the yearning that billowed up from her core. "I want to marry you, Daphne."

His kiss was like dark chocolate, laced with a little anger and frustration and, she could feel it in him, desperation. She drank it in, because she was desperate and frustrated and so in love she couldn't see straight.

"I'm ready to send you a thousand gifts, one a day for as long as it takes you to get your head on straight."

He gave her a little shake, another hard kiss then released her. She was unbalanced, suddenly drifting without his touch, his firm hands and rough voice in her ear.

"Remember what you told me at the gala?" he asked. "You said sometimes you have to let love in."

Her scalp tingled and her hands went numb. The tears were back behind her eyes.

"I love you, babe, and I'm not going anywhere until you let me in."

Daphne shook, trembled like a divining rod over water. Finally when it felt as though she was going to shatter from all that she wanted and wouldn't let herself trust, she sat down hard on a tree trunk beside him.

There was a vast stillness in her, a silence so profound it made her nervous. She wanted to reach out to Jonah, assure herself that she wasn't as alone as she felt right now.

But this was what she wanted. This was what she ran out here to ensure. That she would be alone. Forever.

This is your life, she told herself, a low hum reaching out of the silence. *This is what you want.*

No, something in her cried. *It isn't. You want him and you're too stupid to take what he's offering.*

Helen was right—she was making this harder than it had to be.

The hum accelerated to a growl then a roar. She couldn't think anymore, so she just acted. She let those unruly hormones and her sturdy heart and her daughter's wishes rule her—for better or worse. Something deep in her, forged in iron and betrayal, snapped.

She let go of control.

"I want babies," she said and he whirled to face her. "Like six of them." Words fell out of her mouth in a voice that wasn't quite hers. She was running downhill and picking up speed.

He didn't miss a beat, her handsome, smart environmental bastion. He nodded. Solemnly. "Done."

"You have to give me some of this land," she said. "Not much but—"

"Done." He nodded again. Carefully propped the sledgehammer against the ruins of the barn and slid off his gloves. She watched all of it, every inch of flesh he revealed with a starving heart. "What else?"

"I want to go into the city every once in a while, stay someplace fancy."

"Have dirty hotel-room sex?" he asked, with an erotic

light in his eyes that utterly thrilled her. This stopped being so scary. So life threatening. A steady stream of joy ran through her, eroding the rest of her delusions and she felt like laughing. She felt like sunshine and music and cold glasses of milk. This was everything good and right.

"Done. Very done," he said. "We'll go lots. What else?"

"Family dinners with the Mitchells," she said, just to see how far he would go.

"I don't think we can keep them away," he said. "What else?"

She scowled at him, having been prepared to fight. Having been prepared to be disappointed. "For such a tough negotiator, you're pretty easy," she said.

He crouched in front of her and her heart beat so hard it felt like her whole body pounded. For him. For Jonah.

"I'll give you anything you want. My only deal breaker is that I want you, and Helen and those six kids for the rest of my life. If you can't promise me that, then I walk."

His blue eyes pinned her to the spot.

"Why?" she whispered, her great shame spilling out of her, all the skeletons and neuroses, coming out to play. "Why me?" she clarified, unable to reach for him just yet.

If he had smiled indulgently, if he had laughed, she might have stood and walked away, but he didn't. He handled her great vulnerability with care and she realized, this man who'd felt so rejected his whole life, had the same vulnerability.

"Because there is no one else in the world like you," he said. "No one who makes me happy. No one who challenges me and makes me try to be better than I am. Just you, Daphne. Just you."

Oh, that was nice. That was actually the nicest thing

she'd ever heard in her life. All the damage that she held on to, all the terrible feelings that being left by the men in her life had caused to rattle around her body, up and left. Banished under the light of his eyes.

"And that's why I'm staying," he said. "Because I love you too much to leave."

"I love you, too," she said. And then adding her voice to the roar in her heart, she added, "I love you too much to let you go."

He pulled her into his arms, his hands making a mess of her hair, his breath a hot flush on her neck. "So it's a deal?" he asked. "Negotiations over?"

"Over." She sighed.

"You'll marry me?" he asked, his beautiful face so joyous and stunned.

"Yes," she said, smiling. And the smile transformed to laughter that she couldn't control and she clutched him to her, trying to absorb him, to open her heart and pull him right in.

"It feels so good."

"What does?" he asked, stroking away her tears.

"Letting love in."

His smile was beautiful. Brighter than the sun, the only thing she needed to keep her warm for the rest of her life. "Yes," he agreed. "It does."

EPILOGUE

Four years later

"Wow, Mom," Helen said, accepting the pink bundle from Jonah's hands like the old pro she was now. "This gets easier every time, doesn't it?"

"Does it?" Daphne asked from the bed, not sounding convinced. Jonah smiled and kissed his wife, the mother of his babies, the reason he had to live most days. "Because from here," she said, looking tired but slightly drunk from the drugs and the euphoria, "it's not so easy."

"You did great," Jonah told her, still awed by the strength of this woman.

"It was easier," Daphne said, stroking his cheek. "Third time and all. How are you doing?"

He pressed his face to hers, put his hand in her hair. "Like I'm going to burst," he said. "Like I'm just going to pop."

He felt the small burst of her laugh and baby Iris started to squawk in Helen's arms.

"Here," Daphne said, reaching for the newborn. "I'll feed her and you go get the family. I'm sure they're ready to storm the gates. I can hear Garth from here."

Jonah agreed and tucked his preteen stepdaughter under his arm, hugging her hard because he loved her so much, and opened the door to the hallway. To a hallway filled with Daphne's mom Gloria, her boyfriend and Mitchells.

Lots and lots of Mitchells.

Garth, his two-year-old, flung himself into the room, running to Daphne's bed, and Helen moved to help him up so he could see his new sister. Gloria followed, her eyes damp.

But there were his parents. Iris was crying and she didn't even know they'd named the baby after her. His brothers and their kids were there. Delia and Alice holding toddlers. Josie, with her shadow Stella beside her, was such a beautiful young woman.

Only Cameron, who Alice and Gabe had adopted when he was seventeen so he wouldn't be sent back to the group home after his dad died, was missing.

"Everything okay?" Patrick asked into the charged silence.

The earth tipped. Spun slightly.

My family, Jonah thought. Wondering why the room was suddenly on a Tilt-A-Whirl.

"Hey." Gabe stepped up and grabbed his arm, and Max was right beside him. "You all right? You're not going to puke, are you?"

"You can puke," Max said because he'd puked when Delia gave birth to Thomas. Well, after. From the nerves, he'd said. "Puking is fine."

"Son?" Patrick asked and Jonah swung his gaze to his father's identical blue eyes.

He lifted his hand to the trembling skin over his heart. His family in front of him, the sound of his wife laughing, his children talking behind him.

When did you all get here? he wondered, feeling his heart expand. *When did I let you in?*

"I love you." The words spilled out of his mouth. He turned to his brothers, his mother. His father who had never heard the words from him. "I love all of you."

And he passed out cold.

* * * * *

The Colton family is back!
Enjoy a sneak preview of
COLTON'S SECRET SERVICE by Marie Ferrarella,
part of THE COLTONS: FAMILY FIRST *miniseries.*

Available from Silhouette Romantic Suspense
in September 2008.

He cautioned himself to be leery. He was human and he'd been conned before. But never by anyone nearly so attractive. Never by anyone he'd felt so attracted to.

In her defense, Nick supposed that Georgie could actually be telling him the truth. That she was a victim in all this. He had his people back in California checking her out, to make sure she was who she said she was and had, as she claimed, not even been near a computer but on the road these last few months that the threats had been made.

In the meantime, he was doing his own checking out. Up close and exceedingly personal. So personal he could feel his blood stirring.

It had been a long time since he'd thought of himself as anything other than a law enforcement agent of one type or other. But Georgeann Grady made him remember that beneath the oaths he had taken and his devotion to duty, there beat the heart of a man.

A man who'd been far too long without the touch of a woman.

He watched as the light from the fireplace caressed the outline of Georgie's small, trim, jean-clad body as she moved about the rustic living room that could have easily come off the set of a Hollywood Western. Except that it was genuine.

As genuine as she claimed to be?

Something inside of him hoped so.

He wasn't supposed to be taking sides. His only interest in being here was to guarantee Senator Joe Colton's safety as the latter continued to make his bid for the presidency. Everything else was supposed to be secondary, but, Nick had to silently admit, that was just a wee bit hard to remember right now.

Earlier, before she'd put her precocious handful of a daughter to bed, Georgie had fed his appetite by whipping up some kind of a delicious concoction out of the vegetables she'd pulled from her garden. Vegetables that, by all rights, should have been withered and dried. She'd mentioned that a friend came by on occasion to weed and tend it. Still, it surprised him that somehow she'd managed to make something mouthwatering out of it.

Almost as mouthwatering as she looked to him right at this moment.

Again, he was reminded of the appetite that hadn't been fed, hadn't been satisfied.

And wasn't going to be, Nick sternly told himself. At least not now. Maybe later, when things took on a more definite shape and all the questions in his head were answered to his satisfaction, there would be time to explore this feeling. This woman. But not now.

Damn it.

"Sorry about the lack of light," Georgie said, breaking into his train of thought as she turned around to face him. If she noticed the way he was looking at her, she gave no indication. "But I don't see a point in paying for electricity if I'm not going to be here. Besides, Emmie really enjoys camping out. She likes roughing it."

"And you?" Nick asked, moving closer to her, so close that a whisper would have trouble fitting in. "What do you like?"

The very breath stopped in Georgie's throat as she looked up at him.

"I think you've got a fair shot of guessing that one," she told him softly.

* * * * *

Be sure to look for COLTON'S SECRET SERVICE
and the other following titles from
THE COLTONS: FAMILY FIRST *miniseries:*
RANCHER'S REDEMPTION by Beth Cornelison
THE SHERIFF'S AMNESIAC BRIDE by Linda Conrad
SOLDIER'S SECRET CHILD by Caridad Piñeiro
BABY'S WATCH by Justine Davis
A HERO OF HER OWN by Carla Cassidy

Silhouette®

Romantic
SUSPENSE

**Sparked by Danger,
Fueled by Passion.**

The Coltons Are Back!

Marie Ferrarella
Colton's Secret Service

The Coltons: Family First

On a mission to protect a senator, Secret Service agent
Nick Sheffield tracks down a threatening message only
to discover Georgie Gradie Colton, a rodeo-riding single
mom, who insists on her innocence. Nick is instantly
taken with the feisty redhead, but vows not to let his
feelings interfere with his mission. Now he must figure
out if this woman is conning him or if he can trust her
and the passion they share....

Available September wherever books are sold.

**Look for upcoming Colton titles
from Silhouette Romantic Suspense:**

Visit Silhouette Books at www.eHarlequin.com   SRS27598

SAVE $1.00

A riveting trilogy from
BRENDA NOVAK

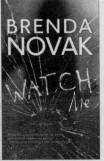

SAVE $1.00

on the purchase price of one book in The Last Stand trilogy from Brenda Novak.

Offer valid from May 27, 2008, to August 30, 2008.
Redeemable at participating retail outlets. Limit one coupon per purchase.

52608328

5 65373 00076 2   (8100) 0 11499

MBNTRI08CPN